The Fangslinger and the Preacher

The Fangslinger I

BRET LEE HART

The Fangslinger and the Preacher
The Fangslinger I
Copyright 2012, 2022 Bret Lee Hart
ISBN-13: 9798818917092
Cover Art Copyright 2022 Laura Shinn Designs
http://laurashinn.yolasite.com
(Revised cover & formatting, 2022)

Licensing Notes

The Fangslinger and the Preacher is a work of fiction. Though actual locations may be mentioned, they are used in a fictitious manner and the events and occurrences were invented in the mind and imagination of the author except for the inclusion of actual historical facts. Similarities of characters or names used within to any person – past, present, or future – are coincidental except where actual historical characters are purposely interwoven.

THE FANGSLINGER AND THE PREACHER
The Fangslinger I

Master Andelko Balas is the leader of a bored, and therefore troublesome, vampire coven in Romania in the 1880s. Colonel Richard Andersson brings relief to the boredom by discovering tales of the American West and setting the coven on an exciting, but bloody, journey to a new land.

Jack Denton, reformed gunfighter, former preacher, now a drunkard, has visions of a great evil coming to Arizona as he wanders in the desert. Then he meets an Indian chief and is given a silver sword, a special cross, and a mission. Jack is led to Black Mountain Mesa where an unusual storm is brewing and he has to face the greatest battle of his life. Is this the last battle for the world as he knows it? Will his renewed faith and special weapons be enough to defeat such evil?

PROLOGUE

Andelko Balas was reborn at the end of the 18th century in the year 1742, in the region of southeastern Europe. His inheritance was bequeathed to him after the murder of his parents; his father was Chandler Balas and his mother Abigail Balas. Their throats were ripped out as they slept by a Godless intruder. Some claimed it was the work of a vampire; others did not believe. Andelko believed, for he was attacked on that same night, but he survived only because he was turned.

He knew who the very old and powerful vampire was, not because he had ever retuned to him in the night to reveal himself, but because vampire blood now ran through Andelko's icy veins. There was a bond between them that could not die. This old and powerful vampire's name had always eluded Andelko, but what he did suspect was this one might be the first, spawned by the Devil himself. The turning made Andelko a leader of the undead, his power unprecedented, other than his maker.

At the forever age of twenty-six, Andelko's human side of spoiled richness lingered with his personality for all time. His inherited wealth had been passed down from generation to generation, consisting mostly of gold and silver. In his human life before he was changed Andelko had been an only child, making him the sole heir to the Balas fortune.

Chandler Balas' great grandfather built Drazan Castle on the top of a great mountain, somewhere on the border between Albania and Croatia. The castle towered high over villages spread far and wide, in all directions. These areas thrived and grew despite the disappearances and horrific bloody slayings that are the legend of the vampire. For over a hundred years, no one dared travel the long winding road that snaked up the mountain to Drazan Castle, for fear of never being heard from again.

Andelko Balas reigned over these lands and the villagers who lived there; only a select few were changed, while the rest were fed upon, sheep if you will? The women were turned young to fill the castle halls with beauty to reflect his own. Man servants were kept to do the daylight bidding, turned only when their age exceeded that of Andelko's.

This brings us to the present night, in the year 1883.

CHAPTER ONE

In the great hall of Drazan Castle, the Lord and Master Andelko Balas sits upon his bronze throne embroidered with green and red jewels set atop twelve granite stairs, overlooking his coven. The massive cathedral ceilings flicker with torchlight. The large windows of this dwelling have been boarded up for many years, keeping any signs of the day from entering.

The human servants of the night obediently serve the red wine to the fanged patrons, careful to avoid irritating them in fear of becoming the night's main course. The echoes of discussion can be heard throughout the room. Andelko zeros in on Thomas, conversing with Elizabeth at the back of the hall.

They have forgotten there is no distance within the walls that Andelko's hearing cannot reach.

"The humans outnumber us greatly on this earth," explained Thomas. "Why we do not turn enough of them to our side to defeat their armies is beyond me."

"Thomas, darling, you know as well as I do too many vampires roaming about would deplete our food supply. I don't know about you, but this girl cannot live on livestock alone."

"Yes, Elizabeth, I understand the repercussions of wiping out the human race. Before I was turned, I was a warrior protecting these lands from invasion. But now, I have spent the last one hundred-twenty-four years chasing screaming humans usually too frightened to fight back. And if that is not bad enough, our leader, with all due respect, sends only a few of us out on rotation to round them up and bring them back here, only on occasion to feed. There is no hunt. I am just pronouncing that the thrills of the vampire are bleak at this time and in this place."

Elizabeth sipped her wine and moved from Thomas' side and then turned to face him.

"Careful, Thomas," warned Elizabeth. "Our Lord is giving us his full attention, and I have no doubt within these walls his hearing has no bounds."

Thomas leaned to one side and peered around Elizabeth by making eye contact with his maker, and then with a slight nod of his head he explained in a normal speaking voice, "Forgive me, Andelko. It is not I complaining, it must be the wine talking." Thomas' explanation exhumed laughter from Elizabeth.

"Do you know how much wine a vampire must consume to reach euphoria, Thomas?"

"I know the blood to grape ratio in this wine is exquisite, and I may have started a bit early this night."

With Thomas' excuses complete, Elizabeth's smile revealed her fangs as they both toasted Andelko from across the room.

Without a response, Andelko turned his attention away from them; by his right he should punish Thomas for his slight blaspheme, but his assumptions were accurate, the vampires in this covenant were becoming weak from redundancy.

A manservant with a bronze tray in hand walked the throne steps to Andelko's side.

"More wine, My Lord?" asked the man, making sure not to make eye contact.

With a slight wave of his hand, Lord Andelko replied, "I'm bored with wine. Find Colonel Richard and send him to me."

"Yes, My Lord." The manservant hurried down the steps being extremely careful not to upset the tray of blood wine, remembering what had happened to a servant not so long ago when a full tray of the thick red liquid hit the floor in the center of the great hall. Vampires were on the server in a blur of an instant; his throat was ripped out to the point of decapitation.

Andelko had felt this unrest coming long before the vampires under his rule; the frenzy that ensued further proof of the tension from the inaction of the coven.

Deep in thought which blocked out his surroundings, Andelko was interrupted by a most familiar and trusted voice.

"You needed me?"

"You know I have always needed you, Richard."

"Thank you, yes, I know. What do you desire on this fine evening?"

"Fine evening – this is a replay of every evening for the last one hundred years. This Coven needs change," said Andelko in his always steady and reasonable voice.

"Would you like me to bring forth tonight's festivities right away? They have been captured and prepared."

"No, Richard, I think not. Release them at the edge of the forest."

"I beg your pardon?" asked Richard with surprise. "Andelko, the people we took from the village suspect they were abducted by vampires, if you release them they will have stories to tell."

Andelko turned his head to make eye contact for the first time during their conversation.

"Richard, you are my oldest and dearest friend since childhood, since before I was turned. Have I not slowed down your aging process over these many years by injecting my blood with yours but not turning you and allowing you to maintain your humanity? By your request, I might add."

"Yes, Andelko, you are also my oldest and dearest friend, but may I remind you that you need me to remain human so I can do your bidding in the daylight hours. The small amount of vampire blood that does run through my veins makes it somewhat painful in bright sunlight. I suppose it is my destiny to serve you, it is also my destiny to advise you, and my advice that I now give is that you relent from this last request."

Andelko pointed his bony finger with the long nail at Richard, clearly aggravated, and with a guttural voice that could only be described as coming from the bowels of Hell...

"Do as I command!" There was a pause and then Andelko continued, going back to his normal tone, "I grow tired of your banter. Give the abductees another dose of opiates and spread them out at the edge of the forest – leave them there, alive. I am going to retire to my quarters; I trust I have an assortment of new literature to read?"

Richard was still a little shocked and concerned with Andelko's outburst, but he calmly replied, "Yes, My Lord, it is so, and it will be done."

"Don't patronize me, Richard, the way you do. I'm not in the mood. Now leave me and tend to your duties."

Richard left his master's side and walked down the steps to fulfill his wishes.

Andelko stood, catching the attention of all in the room. They tipped their heads in acknowledgement as he walked, almost floating down the stairs and to the center of the room.

"Enjoy the rest of the night," he said, hands outstretched and with a slight bow. Andelko then continued up another staircase that led to the upstairs rooms, his cape levitating just off the ground as he left the great hall.

Andelko felt some relief at being away from the monotony of the gathering; he looked forward to escaping his thoughts with a new book. He hoped there was something more adventuress happening in the pages of his new literature compared to what went on in his Castle night after night.

He entered the lavish room that had been his since birth; the one place he felt at ease. Vampires at his level of power did not feel fear, but they did feel restlessness. He lit a reading torch; done out of habit more than necessity, for the un-dead had extremely good night vision. Andelko sat at his reading desk next to the two-foot high pile of new books that Richard had searched far and wide to bring to him; as long as he had dwelt on this earth as a vampire, he read books faster than they could be written.

He grabbed the first book on top and read the cover, *French Poetry.* He set it back on the top of the pile and slid the second book out. *European Philosophy* – with a disgusted growl, he set this book on top of the pile once again and slid a third book out, it read *The Politics of Europe.* With a fit of rage and one sweep of his arm, he sent the stack of books across the room leaving some of them imbedded in the stone wall.

"Why on this earth," Andelko screamed, "can I not get some fresh literature in this cursed country?" He burst out through the bronze door of his master bedroom, the crash resounded throughout Drazan Castle.

"Richard! Your presence is required immediately." growled the vampire.

Richard had taken care of the night's business and was settling down to sleep for a few hours before his day business began. Taking care of vampires required working night and day and he had not seen the inside of his eyelids in sometime. Hearing the master of the house bellowing made Richard roll out of his bed and to his feet in a rocking motion. *What now?* He thought, *this place is going to hell and we are halfway there, I believe. At least, it will be a short trip.*

For Andelko's convenience, Richards' room was located directly across the hall from his. Richard opened his door expecting his friend and master to be standing impatiently in the hallway, but he was not, and his door was closed. He looked left and then right; he could see that the long wide hallway was empty. He wondered if he might be dreaming, until he placed the vampire. Richard was connected to Andelko as a result of small doses of blood transfusions over many years. He could sense his friend and master's needs, like twin siblings might. Richard was careful not to dwell too deeply into the soullessness of the vampire in fear of going mad.

He crossed the hall and stood in front of the door. There was no need to knock for Andelko knew he was there.

"Enter at your own peril." warned a voice from the other side of the door.

Rolling his eyes a bit, Richard entered the room and closed the heavy bronze door behind him.

"You bellowed?"

"*You bellowed* is not an acceptable response, Richard." insisted Andelko.

"Must we do the Master thing when we are alone? Everyone here knows who runs the Castle," Richard said irritably.

Seated at what remained of the pile of books, Andelko continued, "We are like brothers, Richard, but if you were to talk to me like this in the presence of the coven, I would have to punish you severely, at the very least."

"I understand, Great One. I am tired, and being mostly human I need my rest to serve and protect you to the best of my ability."

While Richard was finishing his sentence in this grueling conversation, he noticed two books protruding from the stone wall to his left.

"Is the literature not to your liking this evening?" he asked.

"No, it is not," replied Andelko. "For years you have been bringing me the same drivel. I need something new and exciting, something from...America... perhaps."

"You want me to sail to America?" Richard asked.

"Of course not. Travel outside Croatia or Romania if you must, but bring me something intriguing."

"As you wish, I will leave in the morning. Captain John Beliean is my head of day security; he will be in charge until my return. But there will be no one here to attend to your needs in the night."

"I am the most powerful vampire of this time," Andelko explained. "I can take care of myself and any other matters that arise."

"Very well, my friend," said Richard, with his hand on the door latch preparing his exit. "By the way, My Lord, the villagers were released as ordered, and I will say the vampires of this Castle are not pleased."

"I can handle this coven. You just concentrate on your journey, and I will see you on your return."

With a slight bow of his head, Richard retired to his quarters for some much needed rest before his journey. He had no difficulties leaving this place – infact, he relished the idea.

◆❖◆

With the vampires of Drazan Castle in lock down and Richards's cautious and extremely boring advice at rest, Andelko went on a hunting spree that night, such as had not been done in many years. Not since the early days of his takeover of that region. He had handpicked the villagers to be sacrificed that night so he knew where they would retreat to after being released. Flying across the countryside, the master vampire broke his own rules by gorging himself with the blood of his victims, a total of seven – men, women, and children.

When Richard finds out of this on his return, he will be livid. Andelko knew this, but could not restrain himself. It dawned on him that he would soon be going on a long journey of his own. A premonition perhaps, whether destiny or of his own doing made no difference.

Bedding down in the pitch-blackness of his quarters before the morn, and with Richard already on his search for compelling Literature, he decided what was done was done. A new chapter of the legend of the vampire would be written for all time.

CHAPTER TWO

Richard left the castle located on the small Serbian mountain two hours before sunrise, unaware of his friend and master's bloody rampage of that night. He proceeded north down the mountain riding his massive Clydesdale towards the small towns of Hungary. He was armed with a bolt-action rifle and sidearm, a revolver. It was mid-June and warm for this region as the temperature hovered in the mid-fifties. His garb was wool-lined and sheep-skinned all the way down to his wrap around, rawhide strapped boots.

The Clydesdale was two thousand pounds of an impressive breed of horse from Scotland. Drazan Castle had a stable of twenty-six of these magnificent animals, mostly for the security men who watched over the stronghold in the daylight hours. The only time Richard ever saw fear in the eyes of these great beasts was when the vampires came in contact with them. The Clydesdale he rode now became more serene as he put greater distance between them and the mountain.

He suddenly realized he felt serene as well, he could easily ride from this place and never return; but he would not. Andelko would easily find him and end his life, or worse. Richard would do as he was ordered and comb the Hungarian countryside 'til he found some good books for the Prince of Darkness. *Good books, how about 'The Good Book'?*

This thought brought laughter from deep within Richard. *I would pay dearly to see the look on*

Andelko's face if I returned with a Bible. This continued thought brought forth even more laughter, echoing off the dwindling mountains behind him and giving him the euphoria of freedom for the first time in many years.

◆❖◆

The next morning came; the villagers noticed their numbers seemed depleted during the normal day's activity. The merchants, dealers, and their families were up and about their daily routines, but something was not right. A feeling of dread filled the midmorning air. Missing from this day was the least desirable patrons of the people. Fewer village drunks came in search of their morning bread and stew, and not as many trollops visited the physician's rooms. It seemed several people had disappeared once again.

The villagers would do a search for the third time this year. The first two searches revealed nothing; the missing disappeared without a trace. Some said it was werewolves from the dark forest to the east of the villages, others said it was the vampires that lived in the mountains around Drazan Castle; some suggested they dwelled inside the Castle. Rumors and speculation grew throughout the land. The bodies were eventually found in their dwellings, one after another, drained of their blood, their throats ripped out. Fear quickly spread. People vanishing over the years was one thing, but this was something else – this was mutilation and mass murder.

The last known documentation of bodies found in that condition was the Balas murders, over one hundred years before. Since that time, no one had entered the eighty-foot high walls of Drazan Castle. The Balas heirs never left the security of those great walls and were only known to the Villagers through the stories told. Richard and his guards were the only ones who moved freely between the Castle and the outer lands, riding upon their giant horses.

Richard served as the liaison between Andelko and the village elders, dispelling the fears that Andelko Balas, III, although an eccentric hermit, was God-fearing and cared deeply for the people. Richard had a convincing way with words and the gold and silver gifted amongst the community gave much validity to those words.

Buying off the people had changed hearts and minds in the past, but this was different. Disdain spread in the valley below. From village to village, the anger and fear seemed to resonate toward Drazan Castle, as Richard would soon discover on his return.

The people of the Valley were not the only ones growing restless; the twelve vampires of Andelko's coven were starting to question the direction of their master's leadership. The idea of a mutiny was out of the question; Andelko's powers exceeded all their powers combined. They knew this, but vampires were creatures of the underworld and were defiant by nature.

Thomas and Elizabeth were the oldest of the coven, being the first ones turned by Andelko. It seemed the more humans he turned into vampires, the more the bloodline weakened. Thomas was the strongest of the males, Elizabeth the strongest of the females, and so on down the line. The men were more powerful than the women, but the women were more deceitful and vindictive. It seemed that nature trumps all worlds, whether among the living or the un-dead, and knowing this Thomas sought out Elizabeth's counsel.

"There's been seven humans found in the village; they were fed upon, most of their blood drained from their bodies," Thomas explained, as he stood inside Elizabeth's private chambers.

"And you heard this from where?" asked Elizabeth.

"The news has been resonating throughout the valley below, all of the day and through the night."

"It sounds like a vampire has broken ranks within the coven. I pity the fool – Andelko will surely destroy him," Elizabeth said with certainty while she applied the blood-red paint to her two-inch long fingernails.

"That is what disturbs me," continued Thomas, "I just had talks with John and William..."

"What about Barrick?" she interrupted.

"Barrick was the first I went to; he was the most outraged when the drunkards and prostitutes were released to the woods untouched last night. He went on a rant, angered he has been denied his basic instinct to hunt and left to feed like some domestic yard dog. Barrick has a point, and I believe him when he says he does not know who is responsible."

Elizabeth put down her nail polish and stood, turning to face Thomas. "And you have come to me, because together we can read the past?"

"Yes, Elizabeth." Thomas walked over and took her hands into his. "Concentrate with me and help me put my suspicions to rest."

"You know if we dig too deep and too long, Andelko could channel our thoughts. He may not appreciate our meddling. This may be very dangerous, Thomas."

"I understand this, Elizabeth; will you risk it? Will you risk it for me?"

"Thomas, dear Thomas, I will on one condition. You must do to me that thing which I like, when we are done seeing what we have seen."

Thomas smiled. "Sweet Elizabeth, you know darling, I will do that for you no matter what your answer, I promise."

Slowly their mouths came together, there fangs protruded downward piercing one another's lips in a bloody kiss. The candles were extinguished and the room turned black with the darkness; their cold blood mixed while they both concentrated on the area of the past they wished to see. After a moment, they found themselves flying over the countryside at great speed, looking through the eyes of another. They knew immediately who had broken the rules of the coven, but dared not think it in fear of alerting him of their presence.

As they went from hut to hut, their excitement grew as they relived the past night's hunt. They saw what he saw and felt what he felt, as if they were doing the deed themselves. Deep down in their knowing, they both knew they must discontinue this journey, but they could not – the terror in their victim's eyes and the taste of the warm blood was exhilarating, a feeling Thomas and Elizabeth had not felt in many years. Their selfishness could be their undoing. As the slaughter continued in their minds, their inability to break the trance out of pure enjoyment grew – until they suddenly felt a presence.

Thomas and Elizabeth were suddenly and violently ripped apart from the biting lip-lock and pulled from the past into the present. They found themselves being raised off the ground by their throats, locked in Andelko's powerful grip. Looking down into their master's eyes and unable to move, they began their plea for his forgiveness.

Andelko spoke with clear anger, "You dare to delve into my business behind my back and think I would not discover this." He effortlessly slung them across the room; their backs slammed the stone wall. They slid down to a standing position with their teeth bared, eyes inflamed, daring to stare down their master with hissing growls.

"Please, by all means try it," challenged Andelko. "Make my decision easy on deciding your fate of punishment."

Thomas and Elizabeth stood up straight; they retracted their fangs and clasped their hands together at their front, and then they bowed their heads to their maker.

Andelko sat down in a large leather back chair across from his subordinates.

"A wise decision on your part – I am pleased, for I would not enjoy destroying my oldest and dearest turnlings. But you will receive punishment when I decide what that punishment will be."

Andelko rose from the chair and walked to the doorway. Without turning, he said, "Mention this to no one."

"Yes, My Lord," said Elizabeth as she curtsied to him.

"Yes, My Lord." said Thomas as he bowed on one knee.

The two candles in the room relit on their own when Andelko left the room.

Elizabeth walked over to her bureau; she sat on the stool and continued finishing her nails.

"I apologize for putting you in this predicament, Elizabeth," begged Thomas. "I will tell Andelko that I forced you into this defiant act."

"No, Thomas, I am a big girl. I will accept whatever punishment is given, but you must not forget our deal. You know how that thing you do helps my headaches."

Thomas obliged Elizabeth as he had promised.

CHAPTER THREE

Richard traveled far distances in short amounts of time. The Clydesdale could go long hours with little sleep, and so could Richard. Two hours in a twenty-four hour time period was all he needed, which he took in the brightest part of the day. Stamina was one of the advantages of the vampire blood that was gifted to him. He had already been to a dozen literary shops in several different towns and villages, and he was having a difficult time finding literature that a one hundred and forty-year old vampire with an obsession for reading had not read.

In the early afternoon, Richard was passing through a small collection of buildings, which could barely be considered a village, when he passed an elderly man sitting on his front porch. He was reading a book through eyeglasses and wearing a very strange hat. Richard was a large framed man riding the biggest horse ever seen in these parts, but the old man did not even notice him. He might be deaf, but he certainly was not blind, for he never once glanced up from his book as he turned one page to the next. Richard continued for twenty more feet before he stopped the great horse. He turned around and went back, coming to a halt in front of the older man reading away in his wooden rocker. The old fellow still did not acknowledge his presence.

"Pardon me, sir," spoke Richard. "I am curious to know what book would be so intriguing that you would not notice a stranger passing by."

The old timer turned the book to look at its cover, keeping his thumb inside to hold his page. "Forgive me; it's a novel from the west," he replied while looking up at Richard for the first time.

"That is the mightiest horse I have ever seen," said the man. "I have read about them, but have never seen one." Suddenly realizing he could be in danger, the old man stated apologetically, "I did not mean to offend. What can I do for you?"

"My name is Richard, and you did not offend, sir. I have traveled far and wide and you just may be the person I seek, if you hold in your hands literature from faraway lands for which I search."

"I am Adrian Carpathian. I'm too old to travel these days, but there was a time when I searched for adventure in the Americas. On my latest and last trip, I brought home many books, knowing I could never return. I would not part with this book or any I have not read, but I do have some older writings I would be willing to share."

"Did you purchase that strange looking head covering in America?" asked Richard, pointing to the man's hat.

"Yes, I did. It's a John Stetson."

"It's very interesting, I will say."

"Would you like to come in and see some more goods I collected from out West?" Adrian asked as he stood and removed his reading spectacles from the edge of his nose.

"I would enjoy that very much, yes," Richard said while he dismounted.

They walked through the door of the simple home with the old man leading the way. Richard noticed he wore a holstered gun hung from his waist by a leather belt.

The elder talked as they entered. "I hope you are an honorable man and will not take advantage of my hospitality and good nature."

Richard thought to ease the old man's concerns, but he could not speak as he entered the man's home. The walls and furniture were covered with things he had never seen before. There was more similar, but also different headwear than what the old man wore. There where shiny handguns in leather holsters which carried the bullets side by side in rows on a single strap of leather. One wall held shelves stacked with books, but what caught his attention most were several paintings hanging from nails on the back wall.

In all three portraits, the land was flat and green. One picture had horses with cloth-covered carriages, the white men wore the strange hats, and they carried the shiny guns around their waists – like the ones in the old man's dwelling.

The horses were smaller than the great Clydesdales and they were spotted like he had never seen before. There was one painting that portrayed red men with bird feathers woven in their hair, almost totally un-clothed, wearing only wrap around looking shortened kilts of leather and their feet were bare. The Indians looked as one with the horses, riding bareback, and the bows and arrows they carried were crudely designed and simple.

"It must be very hot there," Richard said, pointing up at one of the paintings.

"America has everything," said the old man. "It has all seasons, spring, summer, winter, and fall. It has many different kinds of people as well, like those Indians you see there, primitive, but proud peoples."

Richard stepped closer for a better look. "I have heard stories about them, but I have never seen one."

The old man walked over to the bookshelf and began to browse. Richard was studying a beautiful painting of an Indian paddling an elongated boat that appeared to be cut from the log of a tree, down a gorgeous river surrounded with green trees and blue skies.

"Here you go, son," said the old man while handing Richard a book, and some papers that seemed to be a publication of sorts. "These I have read several times and could bear to part with."

Richard read the front cover of the book to himself: *Pat Garret and the Authentic Life of Billy the Kid*.

He looked over the headline of the folded papers. *The Tombstone Epitaph, Gunfight at the O.K. Corral, October 26, 1881.*

"This is exactly the sort of literature Lord – uh...Andelko is searching for. He is the man I work for. How much for these two? I have silver and gold."

"No payment," the old man explained. "Just bring them back to me the next time you pass by this area and you can trade them for more, like a library, let's say."

"Thank you, Adrian. Now I must return home, but I do look forward to coming back this way and seeing you again." Both men nodded in a sort of agreement.

They walked out of the small home onto the front porch to find the sun disappearing behind the mountainous horizon; Richard walked the few steps and mounted the giant horse.

"Catch," said the old man as he pitched him a wide brimmed hat the color of black from behind his backside. "The books are a better read when you wear one of these."

Richard caught it in flight; he recognized it as one that had hung on the wall. He took off his wool cap and replaced it with the cowboy hat. He dug around in his satchel and tossed the old man a small bag filled with five pieces of silver. Adrian caught it as Richard turned and rode out before the old man could object.

Richard did some of his best thinking at a full run, and he did so now. He knew Andelko would read this small novel and the pages of paper in a short time, and he would soon demand more of these books. This would give Richard an opportunity to leave the palace once again, maybe next time he would not return.

The farther he traveled from Drazan castle, the more peaceful he became; freedom tugged at his heart-strings. It was true he felt weaker the farther away he traveled from Andelko, this would be the price to pay being human again, to become sick and grow old. It seemed natural to Richard, and way past due.

Richard had been gone only two days and at his current pace he would be home in a day and one-half. As he drew nearer, he sensed unrest within the coven and throughout the village. His strength was growing, and he felt grateful, for he would need it for what was coming.

CHAPTER FOUR

The great hall was full this evening after three days of lockdown. Andelko sat upon his throne eavesdropping on conversations going on between the twelve vampires of his coven, as he so often did. They fed boringly on blood wine as was necessary to sustain their strength. Barrick, turned by Andelko at the age of twenty-nine years making him one of the younger males, was conversing with Camellia and Savannah.

Barrick was evil as a man, and even more so as a vampire. For his acts of murder and rape, he was hanged by the neck until dead. Buried in an unmarked grave, unbeknownst to the villagers the man still lived.

He was six-foot-seven-inches tall and three hundred pounds of pure muscle with a neck the size of a bull. His airway had not completely shut off when he was hung by double ropes, allowing the heart to barely maintain its beat. Sensing the use of his wickedness, Andelko ordered him to be unearthed and turned – to be made third in line behind Thomas and Elizabeth and to become the general of the coven.

Camellia and Savannah were the youngest females at nineteen and twenty years. They were beautiful and for this very reason, handpicked by Andelko. As humans they were as innocent as women of the times could be, but becoming vampires brought forth their natural female wickedness. Sex was alive and well among vampires, their blood was cold but still pumped through a blackened heart as if warm. Sexuality was just one of the human urges that remained after they were changed – emotions making them more dangerous than written legends would allow.

Camellia and Savannah walked with Barrick, drinking and conversing. Andelko listened in on them from a distance with his extraordinary hearing.

"I tire of this lukewarm blood wine," complained Barrick. "I had a need to kill in my past human life, and I am commanded by my nature to kill in this one." He moved like a heat wave among the room with his bronze goblet, but this was an illusion for there was no warmth.

"Here I am imprisoned behind these stone walls, a general of a vampire army that does not conquer."

"Careful, Barrick, my stud of a vamp," Savanna warned. "The Master may hear you, and he seems to be most irritable these days. I do not wish to see him take his anger out on you, my General."

"I do not care – it is better to be dead than un-dead if this coven is going to continue in this direction," replied Barrick with his voice raised.

Savanna placed her arm around him and caressed his lower abdomen, as she whispered in his ear seductively, "You need some release my General, and who better to help you with this than I."

Camellia placed her hand under Barrick's coat and caressed his buttocks from his other side as they walked. "I will join you," she whispered. "Surely a vampire as large and as powerful as you can handle us both?"

"Absolutely without question, my dear," replied Barrick with an evil grin. "In fact, I command it as your General."

Bored with this drivel, Andelko moved on, focusing his hearing from across the enormous hall onto Santo and Nevin as Percival walked up and joined them. These three were turned later in life, thirty-seven, forty, and forty-five. These men were strong soldiers in their past human lives, and after the wars of those times, they came to work for Richard as daytime security back in the days long ago. They were turned into vampires out of concern that the three might turn against Andelko when the coven fed on one of the men's family members, a mistake that was quickly mollified.

At Drazan Castle one could check out anytime, but never leave – instead being turned or fed upon, end of story.

"Do either of you know why we have been summoned here tonight?" asked Percival as he sipped from his goblet.

"Only what I learned from Barrick," explained Santo. "An unsanctioned hunt took place two nights ago."

"Do we know by whom?" again asked Percival.

Nevin spoke, "There are rumors, but being linked to the same master we all instinctively know who, though no one dare think it."

Andelko moved on once again and focused his hearing toward John and William; John was thirty-seven, William was the youngest of the males at the age of twenty-eight, but his appearance was that of a younger man. Andelko had made an exception in his case, allowing this male vampire to be younger looking and as pretty as him. William was taken from a traveling carnival where he was extremely talented with horses. This was right at the time when Andelko purchased the Clydesdales from Scotland; his thinking was that William could work with the great beasts, but as he soon found out the horses fear of the un-dead would not allow them to be trained, or even ridden, without a constant takeover of their minds. A decision was then made to use the animals for the moving of the daytime Army of Twenty, a delight to Colonel Richard and his men.

John's turning, on the other hand, was a simpler story – he just happened to be in the wrong place at the wrong time when Andelko was looking to increase the numbers of the coven.

John and William were also discussing the killings of night's past as Andelko listened inn.

"If it was a vampire of this castle they did not travel by horse, for I was with the beasts, watching from afar all that night," explained William. "Besides, they are not capable of moving that fast, even with the un-dead controlling their minds."

John replied, "There is only one among us powerful enough to cover that distance in flight in such a short amount of time."

"Careful John, do not speculate on actions someone may not wish you to know."

Very wise, William, Andelko thought as he listened. *You are as intelligent as you are talented. I shall remember this.*

William heard this in his mind and turned to make eye contact with Lord Balas, only to see him turn his head away from his gaze and move on to Thomas and Elizabeth. Their ages were thirty-five and twenty-five years. They were not speaking and understandably so – for what all the others suspected they had already confirmed and were awaiting punishment. Vampires were not fearful by nature, but they did feel concern, and these two subordinates were feeling it now, drinking the blood wine quietly at the back of the great hall as far away from Andelko as they could get and still be in the same room.

Richard's head of security, John Belien, stood uneasily not far from Andelko's side. With a hand gesture he was summoned by the master vampire.

"Yes, My Lord," John said, bowing his head.

"When do you expect Richard's return?" Andelko asked.

"Not sure, My Lord – tonight, maybe tomorrow, or maybe the next. I assure you the castle is secure in the daylight hours, just as before," John answered reluctantly.

"Relax, Mr. Belien," said Andelko. "Richard has all confidence in your ability, and so shall I."

John cleared his throat just a bit. "Yes, sir...thank you, My Lord." In his late thirties, John Belien carried many battle scars from wars of the past, and he feared no man; but he had never been this close to the Vampires before for such a long period. The vulnerability and fear he felt at being this close to Andelko, he had not felt since the days of his childhood. His desire for Richard's return was extraordinary.

"Wait a moment," said Andelko with his eyes closed in concentration, "There; Richard is close now – just hours away, I sense him."

Andelko felt something strange coming from Richard; he could sense anxiety and a slight weakness. Sending Richard so far from him was not wise; he would have to remember this in the future.

"Mr. Belien, this meeting will begin. Please remove the servants, and then you and your security men are also excused."

"Your wish is my command, My Lord." This was the most welcomed order John could remember receiving; he carried it out immediately.

When all the humans had vacated the great hall, Andelko stood for a moment until he had everyone's attention and then he spoke.

"This meeting will now come to order. Please be seated, my children of the coven."

The vampires found their assigned seats, in rows side by side and across from each other, six by six in order of the status of their turning.

Andelko walked down the twelve steps, almost floating to the ground floor, his long dark coat hovered an inch from the surface.

Thomas was seated in the first chair to Andelko's right; General Barrick sat in the first chair to his left.

In Thomas' row sat Elizabeth, Katrina, Anna, Savannah, and Camellia. In Barrick's row sat Percival, Nevin, John, Santo, and William.

Andelko began to pace up and down the aisle in front of his coven as he began to speak. "I understand the bored restlessness of this coven. For many years I have denied you the hunt of the villagers only to protect you from the repercussions it would bring. The times have changed from the old days, humans are becoming more knowledgeable. There have been reports of vampire killings in the more sophisticated cities of Europe and I have heard of vampire hunters emerging across our country, waging war on our kind. As you all know, I have broken my own rule. As we speak, the villagers of these lands are turning to this mountain for blame – the rumors of this castle over these many years are come to pass. The days of fear and payoffs of gold and silver will not succeed much longer. Their fear is turning to rage and hope for survival of the humans is growing."

Barrick stood at attention. "May I speak, My Lord?"

"You may."

"This coven could easily destroy the humans of the villages below; your great powers alone are without match. As your General, I propose you allow me to lead this fight that I was born and then unborn to do"

"I appreciate your appetite, General Barrick, but destroying the villages would surely bring wrath upon us from all across Europe, and this castle would be burned to the ground."

Barrick took his seat and crossed his powerful arms, clearly in disgust.

There was silence in the room, Andelko could hear all these different thoughts at once, but Thomas' thoughts were prevalent.

"You wish to speak, Thomas?" asked Andelko.

"Yes, thank you, My Lord, what do you suggest for our course of action?"

"I haven't decided. When Richard returns, he will assess the mood of the lands below. Until then we will stay in lockdown, including myself. Anymore questions, Thomas, or perhaps Elizabeth wishes to speak?"

Elizabeth and Thomas both stood.

"We deserve any punishment you decide, My Master," said Elizabeth.

Thomas spoke up immediately by not allowing Andelko to answer. "My Lord, I forced Elizabeth to search the past, she is blameless. I will receive the punishment alone at your will."

"I will decide who receives what – besides no one persuades Elizabeth to do what she does not wish to do." Andelko began to pace with his head down in thought.

"Under the circumstances, punishment may not be required," said Lord Andelko.

Barrick stood quickly and spoke in protest, "My Lord, as your General I wish to inform you punishment must be held; it always has been and always shall be, by your own rule."

"You are correct, Barrick; seize them for the whip of light."

Barrick, Percival, Santo, and John surrounded Thomas and Elizabeth with great speed. Thomas and Elizabeth hissed while baring there fangs, but they did not resist. The subordinates were taken to the center of the great hall and stripped naked from the waist up before being chained to the forty-foot pillars.

Thomas was a prince in his human life; he was the youngest and third in line of three brothers to be crowned king. He was taken by Andelko one late night as he and a small band of soldiers were returning from a great battle. His male body type was exquisite for any time period, now bared for all to see. Thomas was the reason Andelko turned the rest of his male coven at an older age from then on.

Elizabeth was a princess in her former human life. She was taken by Andelko for her beauty and status. She was now topless and chained to the pillars; her milky white, voluptuous breasts were a representation of perfection for all to see.

John handed out glasses with black lenses to the vampires of the coven. He then opened a metal box that held the whip which glowed white. Made of leather, it was imbedded with hollowed out diamonds, their centers contained trapped rays of sunlight.

Barrick stood between the two subordinates, at their backs with the whip grasped in his large claw-like hand. Excitement could be seen on his face, and with a nod from Andelko he struck; the whip in Barrick's right fist lashed one then the other in an overhand motion. The speed with which he struck caused a blur of white light that lit up the great hall.

Thomas and Elizabeth cried out as bloody slash marks in black appeared on their backs.

The vampires were baring their fangs in excitement as Richard entered the great hall through the heavy double doors. He was shocked at what he saw; he worked his way through the crowd of vampires catching their attention. They turned their heads toward him, smelling his warm and mostly human blood. Richard had no doubt he would have been torn to pieces if Master Andelko was not close by.

He went straight up the stairs to where Andelko had retreated to his throne. Andelko spoke first as Richard reached his side. "This is not a proper place for you to be right now, Richard."

"I don't know what is going on…"

"You're right, you don't know," interrupted Andelko.

"You must stop this for the sake of the coven." protested Richard.

Andelko turned his head and stared at Richard for a moment; he then stood raising his arm, his long boney fingers pointing towards the ceiling, "Sojourn!"

Barrick ceased, looking toward his master in anger. The rest of the coven did the same, not wanting the torture to stop. Now that the rowdy mob of vampires was silent, the only sound in the great hall was the diminishing cries of Thomas and Elizabeth. The second Barrick ceased the whipping, their wounds began to heal as if they never were.

"Release them," ordered Andelko. "Eat and drink 'til the dawn, but remember, this coven is still in lockdown until further notice."

Andelko's attention was diverted to the small napsack that Richard carried. "You brought me books; yes?"

"Yes, My Lord," replied Richard.

"The sack is small in size."

"It's not about the size, Master, it's about the quality which I think you shall find satisfactory, at the very least."

Andelko was immediately excited and intrigued as he glided down the stairs towards the door of the great hall. Without speech, he used his mind to communicate with Richard. *Bring the literature to my stateroom right away.*

Richard heard and obeyed, glad to be leaving the presence of the coven as they indulged in the blood wine while clearly showing their displeasure. Richard, as well as Master Andelko knew an uprising would be coming soon if changes were not made. Richard glanced at Thomas and Elizabeth as they were being unchained from the whipping racks; the looks in their eyes were not good as they conversed with Barrick. Richard wanted to be far from this place when trouble came, but he would have to settle for the upstairs, for now.

Richard balled up his fist and raised his arm, preparing to knock on Andelko's chamber door. His knuckles hit nothing but air as the large heavy door creaked, then opened inward on its own. Richard entered the candle lit room and made his way to where Andelko sat at his reading table; anticipation was clearly visible on the old vampire's face. This look always seemed strange to Richard, to see this powerful and evil entity looking like a child about to receive a new toy.

"I can sense your pleasure at what you have found on your little journey; wine?" asked Andelko as he filled two jewel encrusted, pewter goblets with the thick red liquid.

Richard set the worn leather bag on the table and pulled back the drawstring, allowing the flap to relax, exposing the single book and the three-page paper article. He picked up his goblet and retreated to the corner of the room where he sat in a large leather backed chair that faced his master. He drank the blood wine which sickened and rejuvenated him at the same time, never taking his eyes off Andelko as he watched his friend and master glance over the newspaper, flipping the pages several times. The speed in which the old, powerful vampire could read was just short of amazing to Richard.

Andelko set down the paper and picked up the book, scanning it quickly with his glowing red eyes.

"This is real?" asked Andelko, "This is what goes on in the America of the west?"

"Yes, My Lord. The older gentleman who gave me those written pieces has been there many times."

"Interesting," said Andelko as he opened the book cover and read the first two pages in the blink of a human eye. "Leave me now – I want to read of this Billy the Kid."

Richard finished his wine and, leaving the goblet on the table, left the room and crossed the hall to his quarters. He locked the door behind him. Richard planned to sleep for many hours after his long journey. The colonel removed the western hat from his traveling bag and lay down upon his bed. He turned the Stetson over and over in his hands, studying it. Then he covered his face with the hat and began to drift off, not knowing that westerners all over America did this nightly under the stars to block out the moonlight.

Andelko read the literature over and over again, implanting the text into his memory. He could not recall the last time he read something so exciting and different. An evil looking grin came across his cold, bloodless face as he realized he had a destiny to fulfill. He knew what he must do; the question was how he would go about doing it. After some thought, Andelko answered his own question.

This small coven had mostly been confined inside his castle on top of the mountain for over one hundred years. It was time to leave this prison and take over this world.

Andelko left his quarters and crossed the hall, he entered Richard's room. He knelt over the sleeping man. Ripping out his throat and draining him dry of his lifeblood flashed across the vampire's mind; but this he would not do, for he needed Richard. This was his only friend going back to his childhood many years before he was turned by the evil that had wiped out his well-to-do family.

Andelko lifted the hat that covered Richard's face; he did not wake. Andelko studied the strange head covering before setting it aside. The vampire placed his hands on Richard's forehead and inserted his plans into the slumbering mind. Richard's eyes could be seen under his lids, moving from side to side very rapidly as the information was transferred into his brain. Andelko left the room within minutes, leaving his colonel to dream.

CHAPTER FIVE

Black Mesa Mountain, Arizona, 1885

Jack Denton Anderson was the third cousin of Bloody Bill Anderson who had once been a rebel soldier for the Confederacy. Barely a man at the age of sixteen, Jack had fought side by side with Bloody Bill's guerilla army riding through Missouri and hunting down the Union Army's notorious 'red legs'.

These 'red legs' had raped, murdered, and pillaged southern families across these lands, burning everything in sight during and after the American Civil War. The atrocities that the 'red legs' committed on women and children who were sympathetic to the Confederacy were duplicated upon them by Bloody Bill Anderson and his bushwhackers.

At a young age, Jack Denton Anderson became an accomplished gunfighter and killer, alongside his friend Jesse James. After the war, Jesse James continued his path of revenge and wrong doings, but Jack Denton could not. He suffered greatly from guilt and left Missouri seeking redemption; turning to God, he became a preacher and vowed to lay down his weapons for good. He married a proper Christian woman and had two beautiful twin girls.

He went by the name Preacher Jack, given to him by his small congregation in New Mexico. He had buried the name Anderson in the past, going by the name Jack Denton in fear of being discovered by the law, or the lawless. It was a simple life he now led, and a good life for Preacher Jack, until God's plan for him continued forward. When his wife and daughter died from disease that swept through the small Mexican village, Jack lost his faith in God and left New Mexico, wandering aimlessly, not caring if he lived or died. Forty-year old Jack Denton, a fallen preacher, was now a faithless drunkard living off whiskey – his only thoughts were of drinking himself to death.

Jack had sold all of his valuables, keeping only the clothes on his back along with his horse and buggy. With little food and many cases of whiskey, Jack rode out aimlessly into the desert, drinking as he went. He did not plan to survive the week.

Forty days and forty nights into his journey of despair, Jack found refuge in an abandoned mining shack to get some rest. A vision appeared to him as he slept, the drunken haze in which he slumbered left him, allowing the vivid images of his dream to come forth...

FLASH... A line of men appeared riding massive stallions through a dark and mountainous terrain, warriors of a faraway wasteland moving east in the night, a sense of evil surrounded this army. There were great horses pulling large covered wagons with cargo unknown. Jack suddenly found himself standing in the path of the soldiers, bringing them to an abrupt halt. He could not move, he could not run, and he could not awaken. Panic began to set in on him as beads of sweat slid down his cheeks; his eyes and ears seemed to be the only parts of his body that were working, which he regretted.

Jack heard a flapping sound just before he saw a black shadow descending upon him from the wicked sky. Fear overwhelmed him as something that Jack could only describe as a demon straight from hell swooped down on top of him, baring bloody fangs to devour his flesh.

Jack Denton awoke with a scream from the dirt floor of the mining shack. He jumped to his feet and bounced off two of the walls before settling at a standstill in one of the corners of the room. After scanning the small area and finding it empty, he bent and reached to the ground, searching. Bringing up an uncorked bottle of whiskey, he drank it dry, barley taking a breath. The fallen preacher made his way outside through the wooden door of the shack by kicking it open with his boot and breaking the bottom hinge.

Jack took three steps, and then stopped dead in his tracks not believing what he was seeing. There in the moonlight were twelve Indians lined up in front of him, side-by-side on horseback, staring down at him from not more than twelve paces away. Jack put his hands out and closed his eyes, he then put his chin up, and his head back.

"Well, it's about damn time," he said with a slight slur.

Nothing happened, no action taken, and no words were spoken back to him. Jack opened his eyes and looked left to right and then settled on the Indian in the center – clearly the chief by the white feathered headdress he wore. He dropped his arms lazily to his side.

"Well, what are you waiting for? Kill me."

The wind suddenly picked up, blowing from east to west as the chief spoke, "The spirit speaks to you, you must listen."

Jack had a befuddled look on his face, "What the hell kinda' Injuns are yah?"

"The Spirit speaks to you, you must listen." said the chief once again. He then guided his horse with a pull on the reins and began walking it away. The braves did the same, following their leader one by one in an orderly line.

Jack stood and watched them until they disappeared into the darkness; he wondered if he was still dreaming.

"I need a drink," he said aloud to no one, since he was now clearly alone. The fallen preacher turned toward the dilapidated shack, preparing to seek out another whiskey bottle when he was struck with awe as he glanced upward. There, towering behind the dwelling, stood Black Mesa Mountain, or as the Indians called it, Black Mountain.

Jack was taken aback that he did not see this mountain when he had arrived. Miles and miles he had traveled without seeing it. He realized for the first time where he ended up; he had somehow wandered into the Arizona Valley.

Jack woke inside the mining shack at sunrise. He was usually too drunk to wake before noon, but with all the excitement last night, he'd had difficulty getting the whiskey down. He found his appetite had returned as it poked and growled at the innards of his stomach. Jack rummaged around in his saddle pack 'til he found some beef jerky. He stood in the middle of the room chewing and thinking about the Indians which were clearly a dream. He shivered when his mind recalled the nightmare of the soldiers and the evil that surrounded them.

Grabbing a bottle and washing down the salty meat, he walked out into the morning light as he took another bite. What he saw, he could not believe. Stuck in the ground, tip up – not ten paces from the door – was an Indian spear. Hanging from the chiseled flint point was a gunbelt, twin holsters cradling a pair of revolvers.

What the hell, he thought. Jack stopped chewing, leaving his mouth full of jerky. He gripped the whiskey bottle tight, turned on his heel, and walked around to the back of the building, glancing up at the Black Mountain as he went. In less than a minute, he made his way around the shack and began to chew again while combing the countryside through bloodshot eyes. *Yup, still there,* thought Jack as he walked over to the hanging guns.

He switched the whiskey bottle to his left hand and with his right he pulled out one of the revolvers. The nickel-plated, .45 caliber, single-action Army Colt felt good in his grasp. He turned it over several times; a flash appeared in his mind making him back up a few steps. Clearer than a moving photograph, he saw the fanged demon from his dream descending upon him from the black sky. Not understanding what was happening to him; Jack snatched up the gunbelt and quickly entered the shack, slamming the door behind him.

He was now standing in a dark room full of shadows; the only light was from the rays of the sun filtering through the open seams in the wooden planks. The image from hell left him, but it felt worse inside to Jack than it had outside. He picked up what little belongings he had and left the mining shack for good.

Jack crashed through the door; the sun was high in the sky, burning the clouds away. *This is better,* thought Jack. He dropped his gear into the sand, holding onto the gun and gunbelt. He buckled it around his waist and pulled the pistols, spinning them with lightning speed, forward then backward, side to side, and in and out of the holsters, clicking the hammers back and then forward with his thumb. The feeling was good; he had not held a gun in his hand of any kind since the war, where in the end he swore he would never hold one again. But times had changed, and so had he.

I must be losing my damn mind, he thought.

The Colts were magnificent and the weight felt worthy, they were old but well maintained. They were loaded and the belt rings were full; he guessed he had about sixty rounds, give or take. The next thing to do was to see how they'd shoot. Jack went to his wagon and pulled one of the three cases of whiskey from the back. He carried it forty paces to a large congregation of thick Crucifixion thorn bushes standing four feet off the ground. Jack placed five bottles in random spots around the bush, keeping the last bottle for consumption.

He turned and walked out twelve paces. With his back to the targets, he popped the cork and took a long drink. Replacing the cork, he slung the bottle hard and high over his shoulder toward the bush. With a quick spin, the killer who had turned preacher and then turned into a drunk, fired his pistol. His left palm slammed the hammer once and blasted the bottle out of the air, showering the other bottles with whiskey. One by one, Jack emptied the Colt, hitting the remaining five stationary targets. The sound of shattering glass and exploding gunpowder echoed off the Black Mesa Mountain – the silence that followed seeming more deafening than the crack of the blasts.

Jack reloaded the gun. He put his back against the shack and slid down slowly until he rested on his backside. Exhausted, he fell fast asleep in the shadow of the overhang provided by the roof.

Chapter Six

Colonel Richard was on horseback leading his small but Special Forces army numbered at twenty out of the Albanian-Croatian Mountains for the last time. Captain John Beliean was second in command and Richard's reliable friend. He was a great soldier like all the others who rode this night, but he was much smarter in tactical warfare and a natural leader. John rode side by side with Richard at the front of the long line of warriors and their massive Clydesdales; all the men were armed to the teeth with rifles, swords, and daggers. There was very little talk in the ranks; the only sounds heard were the leather and metallic clanking of the saddles, their weapons, and the thud of the hooves of the largest horses ever bred. There wasn't any snow this time of year, but it was never warm in these lands. The breath of the giant beasts they rode could be seen escaping their nostrils along with the sounds of the snorts and an occasional neigh. There were three wagons in the middle of the line, protected by the men in the front and the rear. The wagons held supplies for the long journey, but more importantly, housed thirteen coffins for their masters.

Twelve nights ago, Andelko put his plans into the dreams of one Richard Duke Andersson, the master vampire's oldest living acquaintance. Richard woke in astonishment that morning; his master's design was very bold, possibly insane. Richard spent the next week working out the logistics for the move that would take them halfway across the world. At first he did not think it would be possible, but the more he researched the more likely it became.

John Beliean, a map expert, was vital in the research strategy for their quest. The two men shared an unmentioned secret, stored away deep in their minds. America was called the land of the free and where they were headed, far away from this Godless country; the problem was they were escorting the evil with them. Both men knew they must conceal their thoughts of escape from the vampires deep in their conscience or they would surely face a horrific death.

Colonel Richard Duke and Captain John Beliean conversed with one another as they maneuvered the Army through the mountains.

"Give me a status on our progress, Captain."

"We are right on schedule, sir; we should reach the caves an hour before dawn."

"Good," replied Richard. "The less the coven has to use the coffins the better."

"Where are the vamps, sir?" asked John.

"Andelko said he had some business to take care of in town."

"You don't mean...? The only reason they would go to a town—"

"There is nothing to be done for them, Captain." Richard cut him off before he could finish. He knew where John's thoughts were going, but he did not want it spoken aloud. "Not even God can help them now."

Drazan Castle had been locked down tight, the sixteen-foot-tall bronze, double doors the only entrance. They were secured with a series of combinations and many different size keys that were hidden; only the master of the dwelling knew of their whereabouts.

Andelko and his twelve disciples of evil stood outside the castle, preparing for their last conquest in these lands. They must feed, engorging themselves with nourishment for the great journey. Only Andelko was powerful enough to fly very long distances. Thomas and Elizabeth could fly in short spurts and the rest of the coven could run and jump, defying gravity in a blur.

While Richard and the small Army of men traveled many miles away toward the east, the vampires swept through the valley into the village sucking the lifeblood from every man, woman, and child who dwelt there. The screaming sounds of three hundred victims would be heard echoing off the mountains for a thousand years, cursing these lands until the end of time.

After the last drop of blood was consumed by the undead, they burned the bodies in their homes to cover the atrocities that took place there. The coven followed their master east, unable to keep up fully. Andelko flew ahead of his underlings towards Richard and the day guards that were sworn by fear to protect him and the coven. The energy he felt from the lives he had consumed was exhilarating. As he drew closer to his army's position, Andelko sensed a presence he had not felt before, a danger if you will. He left the coven farther behind, picking up his pace, feeling the need to confront the spirit with vigilance.

◆❖◆

Colonel Richard and his men were on schedule as was expected from the caliber of soldiers that rode with the Twenty. The journey had been uneventful up to this point, but suddenly up ahead an apparition began to appear. Richard pulled back on the reins, bringing the Clydesdale to an abrupt halt. Richard and John were amazed to see a tall and lean man materialize in front of them.

Dressed in strange clothing, he wore his weapons on a belt that hooked to his waist. The man's dress was stranger to John than to Richard, for Richard had seen clothes like this before – the old man with the books wore such clothing.

The westerner began to speak, but was cut off when out of the dark sky came Andelko, fangs bared and seemingly covered in dried blood. He swooped down to attack the unknown man. The stench of death took over the mountain air as Andelko landed.

The apparition of the unknown man vanished in a mist of white cloud-like smoke. The great Clydesdales began to rear and whinny in fear, breaking ranks in the line.

"Andelko, please," implored Richard, "the horses fear your great power."

With one wave of his spiny hand, the animals settled down enough for the men to control them. Their bodies reacted as calm, but terror could still be seen in their eyes as they appeared to be under some sort of spell.

"Did he speak?" asked Andelko.

"He began to speak, Master, and then he vanished," answered Richard respectfully.

"What about you, Captain? Did the man make himself heard?

John answered carefully with a minor break in his voice, for the smell of death filled the air making it hard to breathe. "No sir, Master, the lips parted but no sound escaped."

The red in Andelko's pupils diminished as his anger subsided and he seemed to calm.

"Put this incident from your minds and continue on to the caves of the dogs, I will re-route the coven from your path to spare the stallions grief."

"That is quite humane of you, My Lord," said Richard.

Andelko knew Richard was communicating in jest which he did not mind in private; in fact, he rather enjoyed it at times. But this talk in front of the captain and the men was not welcome.

"We both know the horses are needed for our journey to pull the wagons. The hulls of a ship will be sealed, but the day is bright in the west and the coffins of old may be needed there. Now, Richard, you have your orders – unless the fork of your tongue feels the need to spew more undesirable thought, I am needed elsewhere."

"No, My Master," replied Richard with a slight bow of his head.

Andelko flew off with a blur, and in a short time, the clear mountain air returned.

"I wish you would not do that when I am around," stated John.

"Do what?" asked Richard with a grin on his face.

"Antagonizing the beast will be the death of you."

"There are much worse things than death my friend, but until then we must continue on."

"That man, when he left us in a cloud, I thought he brandished wings like a great eagle in a flash of a moment. Did you see this?" asked John.

Richard became serious. "I did, and it was a bird's wings I saw, not an angel's, I don't think. A different time may be coming, I believe. Do not mention this or even think it, for you will put us all in danger, under-stand?"

"No, I don't understand," replied Captain John, "and, yes sir; I don't want to think about it."

"Let's move out!" yelled Richard to his Twenty.

The sounds of the great Clydesdales hooves echoed through the canyons unlike any other army had before them.

CHAPTER SEVEN

Jack's eyelids opened slowly from the best sleep he could ever remember having. He had peacefully slept the day away, dreamless and deep. To Jack, time and space seemed to be out of whack, somehow. The sun was on its way down, sinking into the sand, and a coyote yelped off in the distance preparing for the hunt. Jack scanned the countryside; the howl of the coyote was answered by another as an owl hooted while flying overhead, searching for its next meal. He stood and brushed the dirt from his clothing then turned toward the building he'd been leaning against, feeling the unaccustomed weight of his newly found guns that hung from his waist.

He became aware that the sounds of the night had gone suddenly still and quite. Jack felt a presence behind him. He pulled his pistols and spun around quickly, hammers cocked. Staring back at him from their saddles were the twelve Indians, lined up just as they had been the night before. Jack thought he had gone deaf – he could see the horses shifting around as they stood before him, but there was no sound coming from their movements.

An image of a whiskey bottle entered Jack's thoughts. He needed a drink more than ever, and he figured he was losing his mind. His guns were still drawn, pointing at the warriors. Searching their faces for fear, he saw none. Jack released the hammers and cradled the weapons; he looked to the leader; for it was his move. As the chief spoke, the sounds of the world returned, making Jack wince.

"Come, Jack Denton Anderson, for the time is near."

"How do you know my name, Chief?"

"The Spirit has shown me many things; it is time for you to see what you must, for it is your destiny."

"You got the wrong guy, Chief," explained Jack. "I'm a beaten man, a soulless wanderer searching for an end to my misery."

"Come with me, Preacher, and you will find what you seek."

"All right, Chief, you got your ways of doin' things; I'll play along, Hell, I got nothin' else better to look forward to."

Jack loaded his wagon and followed the Navajo warriors willingly. He was not surprised that they were heading straight for the Big Mountain. A chill shivered through his spine as he gazed upon it. He was going there to die, which he did not fear; but the sense of evil he felt would be waiting for him forced his mind to think of God for the first time in many years. He reached back, feeling around behind the wagon seat, pulling a bottle from its box. Jack popped the cork and mockingly cheered the heavens, "Thank you, God, for this meal I'm about to receive." After a long draw, he felt a twinge of guilt for his comments.

He cheered the sky once more holding the bottle high, "Well, at least we are on speaking terms once again, 'cause I'm tired of bein' angry with you." Jack drank some more and he looked toward his guides for some reaction from his outbursts. There was none.

The Indians were paying him no mind, at this point Jack wasn't sure if they were even real, *'cause when you lose your mind, things just kind of run together.*

It took some time to get to the base of the Black Mesa Mountain where the Indian camp was pitched. There was one large dwelling surrounded by three smaller ones; he knew these dwellings were called hogans. The Navajo built homes were wood structures packed with mud with the door always facing east for morning sun and good blessings. The large hogan had smoke escaping the stack at its center. This was the chief s lodge, where Jack Denton Anderson would begin his awakening.

He would have to start his training in the morn, for by the time they had arrived at their destination, Jack was lying down on the wagon's wooden bench seat, passed out from a combination of exhaustion and whiskey. Two Navajo warriors carried the possessed white man into the chief's hogan by his hands and feet and set him to the ground by the fire. His eyes could be seen moving rapidly, side-to-side in a deep spiritual dream; they left him there gladly to deal with his demons.

The nightmare ceased with the rising of the sun. Jack opened his eyes and at first thought he was back in the shack, but the ceiling was wrong. Higher and rounder, it was packed with mud and brush. He turned his head to see the chief eating from a wood bowl.

"Oh, it's you again," Jack said, as he sat up, cross-legged in the style of an Indian, and faced the chief, a small fire burning between them.

"What do you want with me, Chief?"

"My birth name is White Owl, and like you I was born to this earth for a purpose by the Holy Spirit."

"Well, White Owl, I have not seen eye to eye with the Holy Spirit for some time now."

"This matter's not," replied the chief. "Your destiny has already been written."

The leader of the small band of Navajo warriors handed Jack a bowl of cubed meat, while allowing him to mull over their talk in his mind. They ate in silence, which Jack thought lasted quite a long stretch. He glanced at the Indian from time to time, waiting for him to speak.

Unable to stand it any longer, Jack questioned, "Since you see everything, Chief, and I choose to see nothing, why don't we start with what your purpose in this life might be?"

The chief put down his empty bowl and removed his headdress. Jack noticed for the first time that the feathers were from the owl; they were snowy white then spotted brown at the ends.

"When I was born, not too far from where we talk now, at the base of this great mountain, a great white Owl descended from the heavens landing on our lodge. It remained there for three days, unafraid of the onlookers of the tribe. Thereby naming me and setting me on the path of my calling. The battle against evil that you face has not been written, but will happen never the less. You know the evil demons that I speak of?"

Jack, a look of despair on his face, stared back at the chief. He thought back to the nightmares of the pale, fanged creature covered in blood.

"I've had some strange dreams lately I wrote off to bad whiskey," Jack replied. He was trying to convince himself of this more than he was trying to convince Chief White Owl. "I did some unspeakable things during the war," continued Jack. "Later in life, I tried to make up for it, and what did I get – a dead family."

"Your whole life has been guided by the Great Spirit in preparation for this time and for this place," spoke White Owl. "Your inner battle will be one of many in the war of good versus evil."

"Now you sit here and tell me it was all done purposely by God. Well, that kinda' pisses me off. Just what is your role in all this, Chief?"

"We are here to bring you back to your faith, Jack Denton. You are a stubborn man, you will need to prepare for they are coming, and hell is following with them."

Jack stood and exclaimed, "You're crazy, old man! You do what you gotta do and I'll do what I gotta!" He looked around, finding the door, and then headed for it.

"Anderson..." spoke the chief.

This stopped Jack in his tracks; he stared to the ground as he replied in a voice of anguish, "I don't use that name anymore – it's from a time of my wickedness that I just as soon forget."

"You will need this wickedness if you are to survive. You cannot escape destiny, Preacher, and time is short."

Jack exited the hogan and walked out into the morning light. With squinty eyes, he searched for his wagon; he needed a drink badly. He found the un-hooked wagon by the corral of mustangs of the Navajo, along with his own, the stallion easily spotted as it was bigger than the others. Removing a bottle from its box, he pulled the cork with his teeth and spit it to the ground, and then tilting his head back, he took a long pull of the burning liquid. As he brought the bottle back down his eyes opened, looking to the mountain. The flat top of the Black Mesa was covered by clouds without rain. They were not purple but the darkest of black, and they seemed to move in a circular motion stopping at the edges of the rocky sides. He had never seen clouds like these before.

He suddenly had an urge to go up there. "*Shit!*" escaped his lips. Jack corked the bottle and reluctantly put it away, turned on his heel, and walked briskly back to the chief's hogan, pushing the blanket to the side as he entered. Right after he disappeared through the doorway, a mature white owl with an impressive wingspan descended from the sky and landed on the roof of the lodge. The stormy atmosphere over the mountain returned to normal.

CHAPTER EIGHT

The Army of Twenty was right on schedule arriving at a place known as the caves of the dogs an hour before sunup. The men were dirty and tired, but as ordered by the captain they set up camp by unsaddling the horses and striking fires. They pulled raw salted meat from the wagons for cooking and drank water, vodka, and beer to stay hydrated. The men would eat and drink and then they would sleep three to four hours only, this was sometimes difficult during the daylight hours.

The vampires would hide in caves or underground until sundown; they would easily catch-up to the army with their great speed of flight and foot and then move far ahead of them. John Belien, Richard, and Andelko had mapped out their journey with thoroughness; the main purpose was to keep the coven under cover during the daytime hours as they moved forward toward their destination.

Richard left his men under John's command and maneuvered his horse up the precipice and dismount-ed at the cave opening. After lighting a torch, he entered the darkness, walking steeply upward into the depths of the mountain. A feeling of dread came over him as he sensed the evil within. He teetered on a peak of the path that began descending; he turned his head to look back, knowing the small round hole of light from the entrance would vanish with his next step. Richard took a deep breath, and then continued forward, but ten steps into the darkness he stopped, feeling the air turn to a chill like ice.

"Richard."

He turned quickly, his hand reaching for the hilt of his sword as he found himself staring into the face of wickedness.

"Andelko, must you sneak up on me so? I am a soldier, trained in the art of preservation, among other things."

"Richard, my old friend," replied Andelko, his fangs protruding through a grin. "You were steadfast as a human, now thanks to I, you have twice the speed of the living, but do not think you can match me for it would be your undoing."

Richard removed his hand from his sword. "Of course not, Master, I am at your command."

"Good, because we have much to discuss. We will avert off the path; I want to reach the next stop at midnight, meaning your men will have to strike camp earlier than previously planned."

"That is not a problem, sir. The army bends to your will, but for what purpose?" asked Richard, but as soon as he asked this question, he feared he suddenly knew the answer.

"I must visit this traveler of America, the one with the western literature."

"Andelko, he is an old man in a small village. Let me ride out now ahead of all and I will collect all the writings that he holds."

"Nonsense, I will see for myself," Andelko insisted.

"Master, with all due respect I must insist—" Richard was cut off midsentence.

"You insist?" Andelko said, with his voice raised as he grabbed his subordinate at the shoulders. Richard was facing his master, but in a blur, the vampire was behind him digging his fangs into the back of his neck.

The torch fell from Richards grip while he struggled to no avail. Andelco's strength was too much for him as he felt his blood being drained from his body. The minute he accepted his death, unclean power began to fill him as the vampire he called master injected his evil fluid back into his veins. Richard began to struggle and with a will deep inside him, he actually broke free of Andelko's grip. He turned on his master with eyes that glowed in the darkness.

Andelko did not know fear, but he could not understand how this man possessed so much strength. Not even the vamps of his coven ever produced the power that Richard just displayed.

Unlike Andelko, Richard was not just confused but shaken by what just happened, and for a moment he felt hope. Someday he might be free of this evil, the feeling only lasted as long as did his confidence.

"My old friend," said Andelko in a somber voice, "remember from which your powers come, they come from the fallen one through me. You have your orders, we leave after sunset."

"Yes, Master," Richard replied. He picked up his torch from the stone floor and headed back over the ridge toward the exit of light, knowing that the day would be more painful to him from the infusion of blood he received from Andelko. It was a trade-off, his soul for the power which continued to do battle within him, his good versus their evil.

Andelko watched his number one walk away, and for the first time he questioned where his oldest friend's loyalties may lie.

The sun was never bright in this part of the country, but it seemed extreme to Richard as he left the cave, squinting to block the daylight. He walked through the rocky terrain to his horse. His anger grew as the Clydesdale was spooked by his approach, the great animal could sense the change in him. Richard had to grab the reins to keep the horse from fleeing as he dug through the saddlebag 'til he found what he sought. He put on a pair of glasses he had specially made by a villager many years back. The glass lenses were polished smoky quartz, which helped to block the sun. The daylight on his face did not burn, but felt hot, as if he might be running a fever.

Richard put on a pair of deerskin gloves to protect his hands and a scarf he wrapped around his neck under his coat. Great strength pulsated through his muscles and his sense of smell heightened. His men slept upwind from his position, but their odor resonated to him up the mountain. The pale warrior had to fight an urge to descend the cliff and slaughter each and every one of them. He was forced to dig deep inside himself, past Andelkos gift, to draw off the goodness that once was Richard Duke Andersson. He mounted his skittish but obedient horse and headed down to the camp. As he did so he removed the cowboy hat on his head and looked at it, feeling remorse for the old man who gave it to him. Adrian Carpathian would regret the day he befriended a stranger on a great horse, for their second meeting would not be as cordial.

John Belien could not sleep alongside his men, not while Richard was up in the caves with the vampires. John was a great warrior, second only to Richard. They had become friends since the first day he became a soldier for hire. John had survived many wars of the times, but when the fighting ended he found himself wandering through unknown lands aimlessly, until he stumbled across Drazan Castle. If he had known what evil resided in the fortress, he would have ridden on never to return. But he ignored his instincts and applied for work. The day he walked through the huge double bronze doors was the biggest mistake he had made in his life – for once you checked in with the coven of the vampires, you could never leave alive.

John looked up to see Richard riding down the slope from the caves, noticing he was covered up and wearing his spectacles. He had only seen his superior wear them twice before and knew his colonel had been robbed of some of his humanity. He would step lightly around him until he could roam the day uncovered. These thoughts lasted long enough to bring Richard and the Clydesdale to his position just outside the circular ring of the camp.

"Allow the men one more hour of sleep, Captain, and then we move out."

"Yes sir. You good, sir?" asked John.

"One hour," Richard repeated, while steering the animal over by one of the covered wagons. He dismounted and entered, closing the flap behind him. He would rest in the pitch-blackness and hope for rain to keep the sun at bay, for the next couple days would be painful. Where they were headed, he heard the sun filled the sky with brightness. They called America the land of the free and the home of the brave. *We shall see...* thought Richard, *we shall see.*

CHAPTER NINE

Chief White Owl was still seated at his place by the fire when Preacher Jack entered the hogan. He sat in his previous spot across from the Indian with a look of defeat on his unshaven face. Before a word was spoken, the chief leaned over around the flames and placed a silver cross on a leather thong, around Jack's neck. He did this with a finesse and agility that was impressive for a man of his years.

Jack picked it up from his chest between his thumb and forefinger and looked at it in disbelief. "Where did you git this?" he asked.

White Owl reached behind his back and produced a leather satchel and tossed it into Jack's lap. Jack opened the flap and began shuffling through it.

"I don't believe it; I threw this off a cliff at least two seasons ago, maybe longer, the only thing I know fer sure is that I was drunk at the time."

"I was guided to it," said White Owl, "for you will need it if you are to battle the evil that is coming to our lands." The chief stood and walked to the other side of the hogan.

Jack stared at the book in his hand that he had pulled from the bag. He ran his hands over the hard-backed leather Bible; a tear ran down his cheek as he remembered his oaths from the past. He randomly opened it; the top of the page read St. Matthew, his eyes were drawn to Chapter 4: 8, and recited it aloud, "*Again, the devil taketh him up into an exceeding high mountain, and sheweth him all the kingdoms of the world, and the glory of them..."*

Neither Jack nor White Owl noticed the silver cross hanging around Jack's neck. It glowed with a bright blue light for only as long as it took the preacher to read the verse from start to finish.

Jack glanced up to see the chief standing before him, hands outstretched in an offering gesture while laid horizontally across his palms was a silver sword. The sword was solid, the hilt and the blade were one piece, as if molded. The chief strained to hold the weapon, his biceps shook.

The preacher set down the Good Book and came to his feet. With his right hand, he gripped the hilt and then with his left he palmed the blade, relieving the Indian from its obvious weight. To Preacher Jack's surprise, once in his possession, the sword was extremely light. Jack's mind wandered back to the stories of his childhood, the story of King Arthur's sword in the stone. He looked into the eyes of White Owl, searching for an answer to the wonder that he felt. If there was any emotion in that old Indian, he did not show it. This aggravated Jack, but before he could let it be known, the sword came alive with a blue-like flame, as did the cross on his neck. He almost dropped it in fear of being burned. Jack thrust the sword into the ground extinguishing the blue flame as he released it, taking several steps back.

"Chief, where did you git this blade of silver?"

"The blade of light guided me through my dreams to where it flashed every way, protecting the sack that holds the book and the cross and the collar."

Jack remembered the preacher's collar he had once worn. He went to his bag and thrust his hand inside pulling out the white band of faith. He studied the cloth as he turned it between his fingers. Jack suddenly realized where the sword came from; a verse escaped his lips from deep in his memories.

Genesis, Chapter 3: 24, "*So he drove out the man; and he placed at the east of the Garden of Eden, Cherubims, and a flaming sword which turned every way, to keep the way of the tree of life.*"

"Yes," said White Owl. "Only your faith in the Holy Spirit can defeat the Evil One from his impatience. The end of times has already been written, the Evil One wishes to change this and rewrite the prophecy."

"I don't understand," said Jack. "If the sword was meant for me then why do you have it?"

"The Evil One has done well in keeping it from you and you from your path. Time was running out. It is not our place to ask why, but to follow the path to where our faith leads us. Show me your hand, the one that held the blade of blue fire."

Jack put his hand straight out with his palm up, it was dirty but otherwise as usual.

Chief White Owl did the same with his, only his hand was freshly scarred, the palm had been burned horribly. "We all must sacrifice, Preacher, if we are to fulfill our destiny. I was allowed to live to bring you the knowledge you will need to fight the battle for humanity."

Jack pulled the sword from the ground and slashed it through the air; he had learned the skills of a swordsman during the Civil War, but this sword was more like a Gladiator's sword than the thin blade he carried for the South. Jack swung the double-edged blade, pausing only when in his battle stance. This weapon was light in his hands but the chief had struggled to lift it with both arms outstretched. The sword was five-foot long, solid silver; the blue flame did not return.

Preacher Jack decided he would not question the power that the blade held. His faith was returning with all that had happened these last few days. He trusted in the authority that would show itself when needed.

"What now?" asked Jack?

White Owl handed him the sword's sheath.

Jack slid the blade inside and slung the leather strap over his shoulder, he then adjusted the slide buckle which was also made of silver. The sword rested on his back, the hilt sticking up over his left shoulder where it could be quickly pulled over the head with his right hand.

"Come," said the chief.

Jack placed the Bible back in his satchel, he picked up the cloth, and after a moment of ponder he slid it back into the bag. He decided it was not time for the collar to be worn, not until he made peace with his Creator.

He caught up to the old Navajo who was already halfway across the grounds and heading for a smaller hogan with smoke pouring from its center stack. The chief entered by pushing the blanket aside.

Jack, with one hand on the cloth door, heard the screech like a bird coming from behind him. He turned his head, looking to the sky over the chief's dwelling where he saw a flash of white diminish into a low hanging cloud. Confused, but not surprised, all Jack could do at this point was shake his head as he went inside. It took his eyes a few seconds to adjust; this hogan was identical to the chief's but much smaller.

Sitting in front of an intense fire was an older Navajo woman who appeared to be cooking something. As Jack focused, he realized she was melting silver to make bullets. The shiny pieces were placed in a small cast iron pan with a spout that was set over the flames. The woman would then pour the hot liquid metal into a mold. He watched as she dumped a bullet from the holder into a hollowed out wooden log filled with water next to several others. It sizzled and hit the bottom with a clunk.

Jack picked up one of the cooled bullets. ".44 caliber, silver," Jack said aloud. He turned the bullet to see an indentation formed in the bullet, "and a cross."

As the preacher said this, the cross carved into the tip lit up in a blue light for a split second, and then returned to normal.

"Did you see that?" asked Jack.

White Owl said nothing. He had walked away and now came back with two shouldered cartridge belts filled with the silver, cross-cut bullets. The chief handed them to Jack, who accepted them with a nod.

"Save them, Preacher. They may not destroy the demons, but they will wound them. The sword of flame through the heart is the only sure kill; if you take the head you still must pierce the heart."

"Who is comin' – *what* is comin'?" asked Jack, "and how do you know so much?"

"You have seen more than I, Preacher," replied White Owl. "You must open your mind to the dreams that come to you while you sleep, and then you will know what you need to know."

"If you say so, Chief, but right now I need to polish my skills in swordsmanship. Can any of your braves out there swing a blade?"

"You will train at night and sleep in the day, for your toughest battles will be fought after the sun sets," the chief said with the same monotone voice that sometimes aggravated Jack.

This answer sent a slight chill up Jack's spine. He felt a need for more information, so he set off to the chief's hogan to sleep and dream. As he walked across the grounds, he looked to the skies and then to the Black Mountain; all was quiet. The preacher entered the big hogan and set down the ammo belts and removed his pistols from their holsters. He dropped the lead bullets from their cylinders and replaced them with the silver ones. Something told him to leave the sword behind, so he removed it from his back and hung it on a wood peg that jutted from the wall several feet away.

Jack leaned against that wall, sitting upright. As an afterthought, he reached into his satchel and pulled out his preacher's neck cloth. He did not put it on, but slid it into the pocket of his duster. The aging preacher closed his eyes and opened his mind to the nightmare of evil that he feared would come, that must come if he were to move forward toward his destiny. A destiny he now knew he must accept for the sake of his country, and this world.

◆❖◆

Andelko Balas was safely at rest in the depths of the caves of the dogs when his eyes opened, his blood red pupils piercing the darkness. He detected a danger, a feeling the vampire had not felt since the time of his turning. He stepped away from the rock wall that he was leaning against and walked out into the clearing of the natural rock formation. A dim light of blue lit up a small area of the cave. Andelko found he was sensitive to this light; it did not hurt his outside flesh like sunlight but seemed to injure him from the inside. The vampire was not accustomed to weakness and was intrigued by the challenge, but he would not let this flaw in his strength be known for the fear he generated from the humans was one of his greatest allies.

As the blue glow faded, a man appeared – a cowboy with hanging guns. Andelko studied him, from the hat he wore on the top of his head, down his long coat, to the bottom of his boots. There were fear and dread to be seen in the middle-aged gunfighter's eyes, which pleased the vampire. This was a weakness he was accustomed to seeing in the living. But there was something else in the man's eyes that was disturbing – the power of goodness radiated through him.

"Who are you?" asked Andelko.

Jack could not hear the evil entity's voice, but he could read his lips. For Jack was not totally solid, but merely an apparition in his dream. Jack felt this vision was for a specific purpose, perhaps for him to get an idea of what he was up against, to open his mind to the unbelievable.

Andelko was growing angry; he did not like his adversaries gaining any kind of advantage on him.

"What is your purpose?" demanded Andelko, as he paced back and forth with his hands locked behind his back. "Bring yourself forward so we can converse."

Andelco stopped moving and locked his attention on the preacher – his eyes began to glow red.

Jack could feel panic growing from deep inside him as the vampire was drawing him forward from his apparition state to a solid mass. Jack knew he was not ready to face this demon; he had his guns, but the sword he did not. As he was being pulled to the cave out of thin air, the cross of silver he wore around his neck began to glow under his shirt.

The instant Jack materialized, the demon before him lunged forward, fangs bared...

The Preacher tore the top two buttons open on his shirt, revealing the cross. A brilliant flash of blue light exploded, knocking the vampire backwards and sending Jack back to whence he came a split second before the demon made contact...

Andelko landed high, back first against the cave wall with his arms stretched behind him, his long nail-like claws holding him up by digging into the rock. He released himself and levitated to the cavern floor. The cowboy was gone leaving the room pitch black, as before. The discomfort, such as Andelko had never felt in his long existence, diminished with the light. He was excited to finally have a competitive rival to face him and his coven, a war of good versus evil over which he had no doubt he would prevail.

Jack Denton Anderson's eyes shot open; he quickly scanned the room relieved to see the inside of the hogan. The preacher got to his knees, reached over and picked up his Bible. He opened it; finding the last page of *JOB*, he turned the page and began to read, starting at *PSALMS, Book I: Psalm 1*. He would not stop reading until he finished the entire *Book of Psalms*.

Preacher Jack would never doubt again, his faith flowed through him like never before. He now knew his life was for a purpose, as a soldier of God, to fight against the fallen ones' warriors. It was written in the *Book of Revelations* that the Beast would rule the earth for a thousand years. Jack sensed the Beast was impatient to begin his rule, so he sent his demons in a calculated move to speed up his written period of reign. The more Jack studied the Good Book, the stronger he became; the strength of his weapons were only as strong as his faith, the blue light of good was the only chance he would have against this evil of the un-dead.

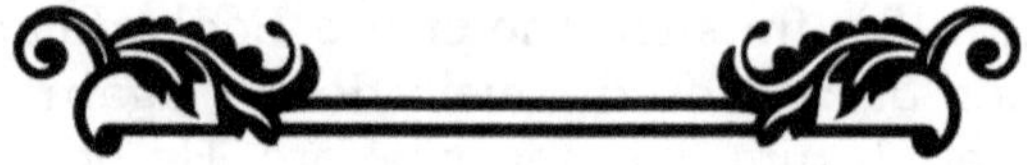

CHAPTER TEN

Colonel Richard Duke Andersson and his Army of Twenty maneuvered their giant Clydesdales out of their mountainous Serbian homeland. The tension from the horses and the men grew as they entered the valley below. The terrain was easier and the air was thickening as the sun was close to setting behind them. The Twenty were the toughest and most fearless warriors in the land, but even these men feared the vampires. Each and every one of them had been looking for a way out since the first day they were drafted into this army.

These men had been killers all their lives, and any morals they may have had in the past were buried deep within them. Even the worst of the worst of their inner evils did not compare to the vampires of Drazen Castle. They knew if they deserted their post or tried to flee, Andelko would hunt them down and devour them, or worse. As evil as Andelko was, he was the only thing that kept the rest of his coven from going on a murderous rampage against the human race. Their captor was also their savior, in an ironic sort of way.

Richard and John Belien left the army in a clearing just outside the small town to set up camp in a defensive position by circling the wagons. Their first order was to unload the coffins, laying them out side by side. This was the strangest of the soldiers' duties, but they were professionals and took their orders well.

The old man on the porch did not notice the two men on their large horses at the first. He sat in his wood rocker, reading and smoking his pipe when he glanced up looking from under the brim of his hat.

"Howdy, can I help yah?"

Richard had removed his scarf and gloves earlier in the day and he had the hat this elderly man had given him in his hand. He now put it atop his head.

"Mr. Carpathian," he said as he tipped the brim between his thumb and finger.

The old man removed his reading spectacles. "Ah yes, it's Richard, right? Please call me Adrian."

"May we speak inside?" asked Richard as he dismounted.

The old man stood; as he did so John saw the single pistol hanging from around his belt. Reacting, he pointed his rifle barrel towards the old man and clicked the hammer back.

"It's good, John, lower your weapon," insisted Richard, outstretching his arm with his palm out towards his captain.

"I would feel better, Colonel, if he would leave his sidearm."

"Colonel?" questioned the old man while looking at Richard. Adrian then turned and spoke to the man with the rifle. "Easy, young man, I will oblige."

Adrian slowly pulled his pistol out of the holster and set it on the porch rail, and then turned on his heel and entered the house. Richard followed and stopped the old man just inside the door; their eyes locked on one another.

"We don't have much time," Richard told him.

Adrian noticed this man was different somehow from the last time they met. His eyes were deeper, colder. "What can I do for you, son? Are you ill?"

Richard ignored his question. "The day will soon be replaced by night. I tried to get here earlier," said Richard with regret. "I just wanted to say I am sorry for what I have brought upon you."

Adrian saw Richard's eyes change back, for a moment, to the man he had met the first time, he put his hand on his shoulder, "That's all right, son. I don't know what you mean, but it don't sound too good." Adrian removed his hand and pulled a match from his shirt pocket. He struck it on his backside and relit his pipe.

"You have a few minutes," said Richard. "I'll leave you to make peace with your God."

Richard exited the dwelling and then glanced over his shoulder to see Adrian go to his knees in prayer. *Wise man,* thought Richard.

The sun had just touched down on the horizon; the turning of the Earth could now be realized as the yellow star had a point of reference sinking behind the far off mountains. As Richard stood on the wood-planked porch, he closed his eyes slowly. He could feel Andelko and the coven preparing to vacate the cave. It took him and his men almost a day to travel here; it would only take the vampires minutes.

John spoke to his colonel from his saddle,

"You left a man, who I suspect realizes his fate, by himself with most likely a house full of guns. Is your friend so trustworthy?"

Richard opened his eyes and answered his captain, "He is trustworthy, but if I was truly a friend to him, I would end his life immediately and swiftly."

John did not reply, but knew exactly what Richard meant.

"With your permission, I would like to take the horses around the back?" asked John. "You know how they spook when the vamps are present."

"Yes, please Captain. I can handle it from here."

John was on the move before Richard finished speaking. Richard knew the horses were not the only ones that were uncomfortable around the coven, and he understood his captain completely.

Adrian lived on the outside rim of the small village where there were a dozen homes spread throughout the modest valley consisting of sheep ranchers and farmers who lived their lives from sunup to sundown. So when Andelko and his coven walked out of the dark shadows in front of Adrian's home, no one in the village were the wiser as they had rolled up the streets and retired to their dwellings.

The old man walked out onto the front porch as Richard finished lighting the second of the two oil lamps hung from nails on the outside of the house. Adrian could feel a change in the night air immediately, his reaction was faster than he thought possible as he picked up his revolver from the porch rail, cocked it, and aimed at the stranger and the twelve others that seemed to appear from nowhere. They were standing in a line on the street as the stranger walked forward.

"Adrian, I advise you to holster that weapon," Richard suggested in a calm voice.

"Nonsense," said Andelko as he glided up to the old man and took the revolver from him.

Adrian did not move; he was not fearful, but felt more like his mind was in shock, or in a trance. The being in front of him smelled of death, he was pale and cold, "*Vampire?*" escaped Adrian's lips.

"Yes, Mister...?"

"Carpathian, call me Adrian. You are real?"

"Yes, the stories you have heard are true. You are in a unique situation, Mr. Adrian Carpathian. There are but a few privileged enough to talk to the undead as most who encounter us do not live to tell the tale."

Adrian looked to Richard with questioning eyes. "Are you a vampire?"

"No, not fully – it's complicated, said Richard.

The old man thought he heard shame in his voice.

"What do you want with me, sir?" Adrian asked, directing this question back to Andelko.

The old vampire put his cold arm around the old man and returned his gun to him by sliding it back into his holster. Andelko guided him inside as he explained, "I hear you have quite a Western museum inside these modest walls, and I would like a tour."

A chill went through Adrian's body from Andelko's touch as he went freely with him through the doorway. He did not see Andelko turn his head and signal the twelve vampires of his coven. Once he did so, they scattered in a blur towards the center of the little village.

Richard followed them inside. He knew what was about to happen and part of him had an urge to try to stop it; another part of him had a duty that he would have to honor, as it had been his purpose in life for many years.

Adrian showed Andelko around his home explaining the paintings, showing and clarifying books and newspaper clippings – he did this not because he wanted to, but because he felt he must. After a few minutes of instruction by Adrian on a particular painting portraying the *Gunfight at the OK Corral*, he paused as he thought he heard faint cries coming from the direction of town.

Richard quickly asked a question, diverting the old man's attention, driving them deeper into the home away from the sounds that seeped in from the partially opened doorway. This brought them to a room at the back of the house which immediately caught Andelko's attention.

"Ah, this is what I seek," the old vampire said with delight as he pulled a gunbelt holstering two revolvers that hung from a large spike protruding from the wall.

Richard saw excitement on the old vampire's face, the look a child might have in a sweets store. The holsters and belt were made of black leather with decorative swirls of white, and studded with red jewels.

The .45 long Colt revolvers were polished to a silver shine.

Andelko strapped on the belt around his waist beneath his floor-length black leather coat. He pulled one of the pistols from its pearl white handle, before Richard could caution him. Andelko touched the shiny metal barrel to his white skin on the back of his other hand expecting, as did Richard, to see burning smoke; there was none.

"What metal is this?" Andelko asked, looking to the old timer.

"That long Colt there is nickel-plated. The rumor is that rig you're wearing belonged to a showman, who went by the name of Ace Hanlon. He was killed in a gunfight competition to the death, which made his guns available for auction – I paid a fair price."

Andelko removed a five-gallon, black felt Stetson from a hat rack in the corner of the room and placed it upon his head.

Adrian could not believe what he was seeing; a demon gunslinger stood before him. The old man touched the middle of his chest, feeling the silver cross that hung there beneath his clothing.

"What does that room hold?" asked Andelko, pointing to a padlocked door at the back of the room.

"That's just a walk-in storage closet," Adrian replied. "Haven't been in there for some time – just odds and ends, if my memory holds."

"You best open it, Mr. Carpathian," suggested Richard.

"I can see I don't have a choice," Adrian said. "I'll have to fetch the key; it hangs on a peg at the front door." He turned his back on his guests and headed in that direction. The old man thought this might be his only chance to run and managed two steps when, out of nowhere, he bumped into a shape that was Andelko's cold chest. Pure instinct took over the old man and he stepped back and pulled his pistol, aiming the barrel at the vampire's gut.

Their eyes locked, freezing Adrian and not allowing him to pull the trigger.

"Impressive, Mr. Carpathian," said Andelko with a grin. "Your lead bullets cannot harm me. Oh, it may sting for a short moment, but I heal extremely fast."

The pistol that Adrian pointed at the vampire had a hair trigger and his finger pressed against it, but it would not pull.

Andelko stepped to the side and put his hand in front of the slightly shaky gun barrel. "Release," commanded Andelko. As soon as he said this, the gun went off blowing a round hole in Andelko's white boney hand. The sound was deafening and smoke quickly rose, filling the medium size room. The vampire raised his hand up for Adrian to see, the clear hole turned black on the edges and then closed, healing completely. Andelko's teeth were bared and a guttural growl could be heard echoing from deep in his throat, his eyes piercing the old man's.

Adrian desperately wanted to shut his eyelids, not wanting to see what would happen next, but he could not even blink. The old man's lips began to move rapidly in prayer, reciting passages he didn't even know he'd memorized.

"Stop with that babble," demanded Andelko, as he released the old man, stepping away from him and creating some space between them, "Your time has not come, for we are not finished here, yet."

Richard had been observing from a distance at the corner of the room. He noticed when this man prayed it had slightly irritated his master. He stored this away in his memories, for he knew he could not dwell on any one thought for very long or Andelko would pick that up and read his mind.

Adrian holstered his weapon, convinced it was useless against this demon that stood before him. He knew he was a dead man as soon as this *thing* got what it wanted. He was still terrified, but now he was also angry. "All right, I'm done playing games now. What the hell do you want from me?"

Richard had a newly discovered respect for the old-timer; he had courage not seen in these lands from the masses. Only warriors showed such backbone. Richard wondered if all Western men from America were this brave.

Andelko seemed to welcome the anger radiating from a man who knew he was doomed.

"What I want at this immediate time, Adrian, is for you to open that door."

"You can call me Mr. Carpathian," said the old man.

Andelko burst out in laughter, a laugh that was malicious and cold.

Adrian took two steps to the left, pulled his pistol, and fired his remaining bullets at the padded lock on the door – five shots, one after the other, slamming the palm of his hand down on the hammer. When the smoke cleared enough to see, the metal lock lay in pieces on the floor along with wood splinters from the wall and the door that now stood agape.

While Adrian reloaded his revolver, Richard grabbed the door and pulled it open for Andelko to enter the room. The old man and Richard's eyes met as more screams were heard in the distance.

The vampires of the coven were very efficient in their acts of mutilation and they had been restrained from doing what was their nature for some time. Now that they had been unleashed on humanity from the confines of the castle their hunger grew, as did their strength from the human blood they devoured. The vampires swept over the small village like a plague, ripping out the throats of all, not discriminating between age or gender.

The Christian people of this place were sacrificed for reasons not understood by man, for evil was making a stand on the earth, pushing to change scripture written thousands of years earlier. Perhaps not all prophesies had been transcribed, perhaps they were but had been destroyed or lost. Or possibly there were scrolls still buried, yet to be discovered. The New Testament speaks of prophets Matthew, Mark, Luke, John, and Peter; was there another? And might he have gone by the name of Jack?

Andelko was delighted at what he saw when he entered the storage room in the old man's house. There was a box holding six lever-action repeating rifles called the 'yellow boy', nicknamed for its brass frame. There were five more gunbelts holding revolvers of various calibers – some single guns like the one Adrian used, and some double holsters like the one Andelko had strapped to his waist. The room held a few dusters like none that the old vampire had ever seen, along with spurred boots and western hats.

Andelko exited the closet wearing a wicked sort of grin, walking back into the room where Richard and Adrian waited patiently.

"Excellent, Mr. Carpathian, I am pleased."

"Well, I guess that's what is most important, now ain't it?" Adrian replied, with much contempt in his voice.

The grin vanished from Andelko's face which pleased Adrian for a moment, but the pleasure quickly turned to dread for he sensed this demon that stood before him had lost his patience. Adrian was an old man that had lived a long life who was content to move on to the next.

"I have seen enough," announced Andelko. "Richard, Mr. Carpathian, join me outside, if you please. The feeding is over and time is short."

Andelko left the room, leaving Richard to escort the old man from his home.

Adrian went willingly, but he did not go without question. "Richard, I sense that you are not pleased with the path that you are traveling on. Sooner or later you must make a stand if you are to save your soul."

"My soul is tainted by the blood that runs through my veins," explained Richard. "Whether it can be retrieved or not is questionable. I do know that a stand is coming, but this night is not the time. I am sorry, sir."

"That's all right, son – don't fret." The old man smiled as he turned and headed for the hall, looking about his home for the last time. He walked out onto the porch to see the master vampire standing in the middle of the street, facing him like a gunfighter from hell. But most disturbing to Adrian was the sight of the other vampires lined up as before except they were now covered in blood. His heart sank. "My God," he muttered, as he thought of all those innocent families, his neighbors and his friends.

A tear ran down Adrian's cheek as he watched one of the evil ones walk over to Andelko to converse.

"This is a waste of time, Master," protested General Barrick. "He is the last, let me devour him. We must move on as the night diminishes, even with our speed..."

Andelko raised his hand, stopping his general. "Enough. This will only take a moment."

Barrick shook his head disapprovingly as he went back to his place at the head of the line.

"What's happening, Barrick?" asked Thomas, who stood next to the general with Lilith beside him and so on as the coven all listened in on the conversation.

"I believe this will be an example of how the Westerners conduct their battles. As interesting as this game is strategically, it's pointless. Even at our speed, we are running out of darkness to reach our destination of refuge before the sun rises."

"I have studied the maps, General," replied Thomas. "We will make it if we leave within the hour."

"I believe this as well, Thomas. As General of this coven, I have responsibilities to all. Andelko playing with his food is an unnecessary risk."

Adrian took advantage of this time and turned to Richard, "You know, son, I always dreamed of being in a gunfight, but this is not quite what I had in mind. May God be with you..."

"Mr. Carpathian, I'm afraid not even the crucifixion can save me from the path I have been following for these many years."

"You'd be surprised, my son, and someday you just might."

The old man walked down the steps of the front porch and took his stance in the dirt road, facing the master of the undead. His open palm hovered over the butt of his gun in wait.

Andelko slung back his long coat behind his pistols, his bony white fingers floated over the Colt handles. "Mr. Carpathian I can give you a new life," spoke Andelko. "You can be the thirteenth member of this coven if you will bow down and worship me."

"Never," said Adrian. "Away from me, devil!"

"Very well then, say when."

Adrian pulled his pistol first then Andelko pulled both of his with such speed they seemed to fire at the same time. The old man's single bullet hit the vampire in the lower neck, striking its intended target. Andelko's head jerked backward and to the side. As he brought it back, a hiss could be heard through his exposed fangs, the cold blood oozed slowly down his chest.

Adrian dropped straight to his knees, two bullet holes in his upper chest. He looked down at his shirt, at the expanding red blood. He turned his head upward to see the vampire had closed the distance and was now standing before him. To Adrian's disappointment, the hole in the demon's neck had already healed, leaving only a faint scar.

Andelko bared his fangs and lunged, biting the old man's neck and sucking out the blood he had left.

The last thing Adrian heard was his own scream before everything went dark.

Over many years, Richard had witnessed the murderous feeding of the undead on the human race with little emotion, but this killing of the old man troubled him. It seemed the farther away he traveled from the castle and the lands where it stood, the less agreeable he became with the atrocities of Andelko's reign. He knew he must conceal these rebellious emotions from his master or face a gruesome death, or worse...

"Richard...Richard?" called Andelko.

Richard was pulled away from his deep thoughts, as his vision cleared to see his master speaking to him with the old man's blood dripping from his bottom lip. "Sir, yes, Andelko?" replied Richard.

"My friend, you seem to be on a journey of your own. May I remind you of your loyalties to me."

"I am well, My Master. What are your wishes?"

Any suspicions Andelko had were immediately dismissed when his old friend referred to him as master in front of the entire coven. They were now surrounding Adrian's body at the steps of the front porch, like vultures waiting for scraps. Andelko's arrogance affected his judgment and he instantly dismissed Richards' behavior.

"We must leave this place at once for the depths of the next set of rock formations before the sun arises. Load the weapons and the literature from this dwelling into the wagons, and then burn all the bodies along with the town."

Before Richard could reply, Andelko, with two steps took flight into the night sky, followed on foot at great speed by eleven of the coven. General Barrick stayed behind and walked up the front porch steps, confronting Richard face to face. Richard could smell death resonating from this soldier of hell that was a foot taller and a foot wider than he.

"Master Balas does not see you struggling from within as I do on where your loyalties lie, I suspect. I am watching you, human, and if I see a hint of betrayal, I will devour you without prejudice."

Richard stood his ground and locked eyes with this adversary of evil. "You seem a little paranoid, Barrick?"

Barrick suddenly saw a hint of white light, very faint and very deep in Richards' eyes, that made the General a little unsure of himself for a split second, a feeling he never remembered having in this life.

"You best heed my warning, human," threatened Barrick.

"Yes sir, General," replied Richard.

With a flash, the vampire was gone, leaving nothing but a blur behind. Richard went around to the back of the house, to where John Belien had led the horses in an attempt to keep them calm.

"John?"

"That was interesting," John commented from his place in the dark where he stood between the two Clydesdales.

"You saw?" asked Richard.

"I saw enough, Colonel."

"Strike the camp and procure the men, I need the half-empty wagon brought to me here with two men for loading. You take the rest and sweep the town from front to back and burn everything. Make sure what's left of the bodies are inside their homes, we don't want any of them turning."

"Are those your orders, Colonel?" asked John.

"Is there a problem, Captain?" Richard asked with a hint of irritation in his voice.

"May I have permission to speak freely, sir?"

"Yes, John, permission granted. But might I remind you that time is a factor."

"What are we doing here, Richard; this is not work for a soldier, cleaning up these demons' mess. There was no battle here, this was a massacre."

"Watch your tongue, my friend. You knew the minute you stepped foot inside that mountain castle you were recruited into an army from which there was no turning back. If you or any of the men refuse any orders given there's the road. I won't stop them or you." Richard left his arm up in a dramatic pose for a moment, pointing in the opposite direction from which they were heading while giving his captain ample time to reply.

John stared at his commander without a word.

Richard continued, "You know as well as I do any deserters would not get far. Andelko would hunt them down and kill them in a manner worse than any death a human could imagine."

John handed Richard the reins to his horse and with some effort mounted his. "As much as I don't like it," said John, "as usual you are right. Consider it done; we will be ready to move out in one hour."

The captain rode off towards the camp; the ground shook from the pounding hooves of the large beast only subsiding with as his distance increased.

Richard walked his horse to the front porch and tied him off to the post. He looked to the street and regarded Adrian Carpathian's blood deprived body for an instant before entering his home. Richard went straight to the storage room and removed from the wall a gunbelt holding two steel frame .44 caliber Remington revolvers and buckled them to his waist.

He figured in order to play this cowboy game he best be dressed for the part. The guns felt like they belonged there, hanging down from his hips, as comfortable as a worn pair of boots. Richard pulled the steel and checked the cylinders; they were loaded, as were all the guns in Adrian's house. Almost like the old man was expecting trouble, but his premonition did not go far enough – for if it had, he would have had the guns loaded with silver bullets instead of lead.

The wagon pulled up with two of the eldest soldiers at the helm. Richard had no doubt they had volunteered for the loading duty. These seasoned vets had cleaned up the coven's messes before and would rather haul crates then bodies. Richard returned to the front porch and took a seat in the old man's rocker, lit a hand-rolled cigar, and watched as the men went back and forth loading the wagon.

The rest of the army passed by, heading into the small village; two of the soldiers at the rear stopped and rolled up what was left of the old man's body into a burlap covering and dragged it by rope to where the remnants of the townspeople would be stacked for burning.

John dismounted and climbed the porch steps and stood before his commander, taking notice of the new weapons while he presented his report.

Richard was watching the wrapped body of the old man being dragged along the ground by his feet as he smoked.

"I took the liberty of amassing the bodies to the church at the center of the village for cremation."

"I never took you for a religious man, Captain," replied Richard.

"Between you and me, sir, there is no honor in what we do, evil has taken over these lands, and I fear we are on the wrong side of this battle for humanity."

"I understand, John. What I need to know is will you be able to do your duty?"

"Yes sir, Colonel. At this time, I see no way out. Maybe these new lands in the West will be different. I will have your back, Richard, like I always have."

Richard stood and put his hand on his captain's shoulder. "Thank you, John. Let's get this done; we have a schedule to keep."

"Yes sir, Colonel, right away."

Richard was not done conversing with his captain when he was interrupted by the two men coming out of the house.

"Captain, Colonel," said the soldier with a quick salute that was not returned by either superior. This was not regular army, but for the seasoned warrior old habits were hard to break. "That's the last of it."

"Right, soldier," said John. "Move the wagon to the south, just outside of town and wait there. We will be there shortly."

"Yes sir." The men enthusiastically jumped onto the bench seat of the wagon. With a *yah* and a slap of the reins, they were headed down the dirt road, clearly relieved they were not ordered to help the others with the unpleasant task of scorching the innocent souls of this small township.

"I'll torch the old man's home myself, Captain," said Richard, as he tapped on the porch rail with his forefinger. "Order the men to work their way back and set fire to the rest. And, John, you must control your thoughts around the vampires, especially Andelko, or you will never see this place called America."

"I understand, sir," replied John. "Make sure you heed your own advice – with Andelko's blood running through your veins, his connection with your thoughts could be extremely dangerous for all of us."

With that said, the once proud warriors went on with their forced duties, able to do so only from many years of practiced discipline over their conscience. Guilt was an emotion a soldier could not afford to have, but a good soldier must have honor and all the Twenty knew that the work they did for the vampires was not honorable.

Richard had handpicked each one of the men in his army and knew they would follow him to hell and back – which was exactly where he feared they were headed.

CHAPTER ELEVEN

The vampires who had lived in the mountains of Romania and Croatia for hundreds of years were now migrating to the Americas, being led by one Andelko Balas. Only Jack Denton Anderson had any sign of their traveling progress or any knowledge of their estimated time of arrival to the Black Mesa Mountain. His dreams were the source of his knowledge and he had opened himself up to this information with vigor.

Unbeknownst to Jack, at this specific time he had a slight advantage over the leader of the coven due to vampire arrogance. Andelko did not recognize why or who drove him towards this battle, but Preacher Jack knew he was the downtrodden who had been chosen as an instrument of the Holy Spirit. The honesty, which is of good, had revealed itself to Jack; the deceit, which is of evil, could not show itself to Andelko.

Jack studied the Word by day and battle trained by night. His shooting skills returned to him quickly. Where he was lacking was in his time of practice with the sword. Jack carried a weapon of elongated steel in his youth during the Civil War, but that forged blade was incompetent compared to the solid silver protector of the Biblical Garden.

As goes the sun, so goes the training. Two hours of target practice with the pistol and the rifle, followed by many hours of drill with the sword. There were three braves appointed by White Owl to duel with the preacher; they were his best warriors. The Indians were not practiced in this type of warfare, but they were proficient in the art of hand-to-hand combat, including the spear and the tomahawk. It seemed the sword of solid silver somehow knew the difference between true battle and preparation. Blue light did not radiate from the blade, and it did not fragment the wood-handled weapons that the braves wielded for the training.

Jack was becoming stronger by the day. Spiritually and physically, his stamina exceeded the three younger adversaries with whom he trained at the bottom of the mountain. When a hint of fatigue would creep into him, he would look to the top of the Black Mesa and ask God for strength, while holding onto the cross that hung from his neck. The blue light would glow, illuminating the cross and revitalizing his weary body, convincing him that his whole life was for this purpose all along.

Chief White Owl had gone missing for a week now, leaving while Jack slept. The preacher had made inquiries about the location of the chief to no avail. The language barrier was a problem between him and the braves as only White Owl spoke his language. Jack would then turn to his faith, reassuring himself that his chosen Indian deliverer would return, for he feared he could not complete his task without him.

Jack trained six days and then he rested on the seventh day as was written in the book of Genesis. Day Seven consisted of a morning bath in the river that ran south, giving life to parts of the vast desert, followed by Biblical study and much needed rest. The preacher's sleep had gone uninterrupted since he had appeared to his enemy in a dark cave in a faraway land, materializing from his dreams.

On this particular night on his day of renewal, he had a vision of great tragedy. Jack woke in a cold sweat remembering his nightmare and the screaming of men, women, and children as their lifeblood was drained from their flesh by many demons. A tear ran down Jack's face for the victims of the small village in a land unknown to him. A feeling of joy immediately followed as he was shown that every one of their souls had risen up to their proper places by the Father's side.

Jack had trained to defeat the demon from his dreams. The realization that there was more than one of these vampires was revealed to the preacher for the first time. This drained him of some of his confidence; in fact, a feeling of hopelessness crept into Jack's gut. He knew he must control his emotions, so Preacher Jack went to his wagon and opened a compartment under the bench seat to pull out his forgotten shotgun. He scooped up a wrapped skin full of shells and with a determined stride made his way to the side of the mountain.

Jack knew the Lord does not put on a man more than he can handle. He also knew that the powerful thrust of a Fall and Cunningham, side by side, double barrel shotgun could be a stress reliever. Jack cocked back both hammers and put the break-action scattergun to his shoulder, aiming at a large clump of cacti growing at the base of the mountain. He squeezed both triggers. The *boom* echoed throughout the valley, splattering cactus fragments in all directions.

Quickly, with both hands, Jack broke the long barreled gun and raised it up and back, allowing the spent cartridges to slide out of the chambers. Then he practiced his speed reloading, again he pulled back both hammers, and swung to his left, aiming at another giant cactus. His index finger pressed against the triggers just to the breaking point when, by hook or by crook, the gun remained silent. Perched on top of the cacti stayed a white owl, watchful and proud.

Jack brought the shotgun down to his waist, glaring at the great bird that seemed to be waiting for what, he did not know? The sounds of the desert were eerily still; the preacher did not hear any sound but instead sensed someone behind him. He turned on his boot heel that dug into the sand and prepared to fire from the hip. There, perched on his horse, was the chief. The long-standing warrior had remnants of travel about him. As Jack released the hammers of his weapon from the ready, he noticed a very old looking rectangular gold laden box hanging around Chief White Owl's shoulder by a rope. Jack dropped the butt of his gun to the sand and holding it up by the still warm barrel waited for the Indian to speak.

The chief did not say anything, but just stared back at him.

The preacher rubbed his brow with irritation. "Getting information out of this man is like pulling teeth," Jack quietly said to no one in particular. "All right, Chief, I give up. Where yah been and what's in the box?"

"The boom gun will not kill the undead," said White Owl. "There is no silver for it."

"I got yah, Chief, but there are men riding with the evil ones. And I don't know if you know it or not, cuz you don't talk much, but there are a total of twelve vampires coming this way, not counting their leader."

"Come," said the chief, he then pulled the reins guiding his horse toward the hogan.

Jack suddenly recalled the perched owl, he turned his head and looked to the cactus behind him; the fowl was gone. He wondered if the chief had seen the bird, or if it was for his eyes only. He looked to the sky over the mountain; it was calm today, but Jack knew a great battle was going to take place there and he would be right in the middle of it all. Jack did not fear death, but he did fear failure; there was something big going on here, a move against mortal man that might never be written. The preacher would need the bloody skills of his past, but more importantly, he would need to open himself up to the belief of the Creator if he were to take on such evil.

Right now, Jack needed a drink and diverted his path toward the wagon where he pulled a bottle of whiskey from its box on his way to meet with White Owl. *Loose lips sink ships,* thought Jack. Maybe he could get the old Indian to drink some of this hooch and release some answers that he craved. He reached the door to the hogan and took a nice draw from his bottle before entering. Jack went in and there sat the chief, his legs crossed and smoking his pipe, with that same emotionless stare on his face, the same look that sometimes infuriated Jack.

"So where yah been there, Chief? You know you left me here with not one of your people able to speak my language."

"I have my callings like you have your own," said the chief.

Jack sat down and grabbed a tin cup then filled it half-way from his bottle, he then leaned forward and set it on the ground by the chief.

"We must work together if we're going to triumph in this upcoming conflict," stated Jack.

"I sought out and found you, Preacher, remember?" answered White Owl.

The chief had a knack for humbling Jack, the way he lived his life in confidence and honesty. It was no accident that this man was the leader of his people.

"I hear yah, Chief; can you tell me what's in the box?"

"I do not know what it holds," said the chief.

Jack looked over at the container; he hoped it was another weapon, maybe another blade.

"Did you find it in the same place that you found the sword and my satchel?"

"It had been buried for many moons deep in the earth. The ground shook were I stood as it pushed its way up to the surface through the sand."

Jack listened intently, assuming it was another gift to him from an angel of good.

Chief White Owl seemed to read the Preacher's mind and answered his question before he asked it. "This gift is for my use at a later time. I am to keep it by my side until the time it is needed. This is what the Spirit has told me."

"All right, Chief," replied Jack. "I got yah, curiosity killed the cat right, but now what? My skills with the sword have reached their limit and my gun show is as good as it ever was; I'm just depleting the stocks of ammo at this point."

"You must study the book and meditate; dream, let the Spirit guide you. You must eat and rest, for you will need all your energy for the task at hand."

The chief said this, then picked up the tin of whiskey and handed it to the preacher as he got to his feet. Without a word, he went to his bedding at the far side of the room and laid down for much needed rest.

Jack talked to the old Injun's back, "Get some rest, Chief, we'll talk later." Jack tipped the cup and swallowed down the whiskey. He turned on his feet and took the three steps to his bed; he lay on his back with a rolled blanket tucked underneath his head and began to read the Holy Book 'til his eyes grew heavy. Little did he know that his next move would be revealed to him in his sleep.

Chapter Twelve

Andelko's Army of Twenty traveled by day while the vampires of the coven traveled during the night, taking refuge from the daylight in the many caves and catacombs in the lands that was Europe. The vampires had not been forced to use the coffins that the men hauled in the wagons at this point, which were carried for difficulties in finding shelter. The undead were at their most vulnerable when locked into these wooden boxes. The coven could be burned to ashes without any chance to defend themselves, if done during daylight hours. The vampire's only chance would be to escape the burning coffin and bury themselves into a soft patch of ground, before the fire or the sunlight consumed them. The military men had discussed this strategy, but as they moved further east their opportunities diminished as the rocky ground became more porous.

The only chance the men would have to end their servitude was to burn all thirteen vampires at once. If even one escaped to heal underground, or submerge deep under water, the men would be hunted down and torn apart after the next setting of the sun. The hope of taking action against the predators of men had all but disappeared from the daytime discussions by the soldiers, as the ground was turning soft and they now found themselves two days from the sea harbors of Portugal.

John Belien did not participate in the strategies against the vampires, but he was aware of the talk. He understood the position of the men – like him, they were prisoners, once free men and embedded in their nature to look for a means of escape. The cost of abandoning their duties would result in severe punishments; the penalty for desertion was punishable by an unconscionable death.

The most senior of the soldiers told a tale of one of their own who defied Andelko in a disrespectful manner. He'd been drawn and quartered by four of the giant horses in the courtyard for all to see. Another had deserted his post and by the next morning, his body was found hanging upside down, decapitated, and totally drained of his lifeblood.

Colonel Richard Andersson and Captain John Belien led their Army through Italy, Switzerland, and Spain with little incident. When Richard and John had mapped out their journey, they purposely avoided as many towns and villages as possible without saying so aloud to one another. They both knew the vampires would feed on any humans they came across, as was their nature. The vampires drank blood wine carried in the wagons and fed on wild animals and livestock as an alternative.

On one particular night, near the border of Croatia and Italy, Richard had witnessed a battle between two of the coven and a pack of wolves fighting over several Roe deer. Thomas and Elizabeth had cornered the deer in a canyon. They soon discovered a wolf pack had been running that same deer herd. Richard had just left a meeting with Andelko and came across the spectacle. He was on top of the ridge observing when the vampires cornered the deer. Before they could feed upon them they were surrounded by four black wolves and a larger white one.

Richard, being a soldier in many armies over the years, immediately recognized the white wolf as the leader. He respected the wolves as honorable creatures and was saddened that they would soon be torn apart, along with the deer, by the bloodsuckers that were his superiors. Richard leaned on the saddle horn watching and was shocked at what happened next.

The colonel had never seen any living creature, human or otherwise, physically stand up to the vampire. They showed no fear as two wolves lunged at Thomas and two other blacks attacked Elizabeth. The White wolf paced back and forth around the skirmish, seeming to contain all between him and the canyon wall. This was an intelligent battle tactic often used by men.

With his fangs bared, Thomas caught the two wolves by their necks in mid-air as they leapt at him, one in each hand, tossing them up and over his shoulder and slamming them into the rock wall. At the same instant Elizabeth raised her arm as one of the charging animals clamped his jaws around it and separated her forearm from her body at the elbow. Before she could sling the animal to the side, she managed to duck and her other attacker passed her by without contact.

Thomas and Elizabeth now faced the white wolf with their fangs in full display, the sounds of their hissing resonating off the rock face. They turned their heads quickly as the black wolves were back to their feet and approaching them from behind. Elizabeth's cold blood dripped slowly from her arm as she took flight, followed by Thomas. They both landed a good hundred feet behind the leader of the wolves, and with a blur, they were gone.

The white wolf faced the rock wall as he brought his head straight up toward the ledge and locked eyes with Richard from where he observed from his horse. The white wolf opened his mouth and let out a tremendous howl. The black wolves immediately joined in and their cries echoed throughout the canyon.

Richard's Clydesdale reared with a whinny, eager to vacate the area. The colonel made a mental note on what he had just witnessed; he would give the wolves a wide berth as he made his way back to camp. He would relay the orders received from Andelko to his captain, keeping him on a need to know basis as was standard protocol in the chain of command.

After meeting with the captain, Richard rode on ahead of the Twenty to the harbor of Portugal to secure a ship for their long journey across the Atlantic Ocean. He had no doubt he could lease, or more likely buy, a vessel with the cache of gold and jewels he carried.

The Whaling industry in the Atlantic between Europe and the United States was diminishing and moving to other oceans, some of the older whaling men were not willing to leave their lands, forcing them to abandon the trade for good. Rumors of the times told of harbors scattered with anchored ships and retired fishers of men. Richard felt confident he would have many ships to choose from.

His assumption proved correct when he arrived at Portugal harbor that neighbored with Spain. The vessel he had found was one of the many out of commission Whalers which was affordably purchased. The next problem was hiring a captain to navigate her. Many of the captains were retired due to age or from injury, or had moved on to other ventures.

Richard was a descendent of the infamous soldiers of Rome, as was most of his Army of Twenty. Historically, they conquered by land not by sea; but if forced without choice, Richard would sail the big ship to America himself, confident that with the navigational skills of John Belien he could do so.

Eventually, word got around the docks of a Romanian soldier who purchased a ship with bags of ancient gold coins that was looking for a skipper to sail her to America. Richard was climbing off the boat and onto the dock after his final inspection was complete when he spotted a man walking towards him down the boardwalk. He was an extremely tall and thin man with a foot-long, mostly white beard, dressed all in dark blue. His sailor's hat was the same black as the patch that covered his left eye. Tucked into his black belt was a single Colt Navy revolver, hanging from his right shoulder with a leather strap was a wood stock attachment which could be quickly connected to the pistol for distance shooting. The man was older, but obviously in proficient shape.

Richard suddenly realized as the one eyed man stopped ten paces in front of him, that he, Richard, had unknowingly moved his right hand to the butt of his newly acquired revolver.

"I hear you're lookin' to hire a captain for this vessel?" asked the stranger.

"I am," replied Richard. "You are American?"

"I am, and I have skippered many a vessel, for the right price of course."

"Then you know your way across the Atlantic?" asked Richard.

"I could make that run in my sleep, drunk, or under siege and have done so many times, for the right price, like I said."

"I assure you, meeting a price will not be a problem. I not only need a captain, but a discrete one."

The man stroked his long white beard. "Your dress tells me this won't be a whaling expedition. You know, running slaves to America is highly illegal and risky these days. But I have done that kind a' work, and I know places along the Virginia coast that we can get in and out of by avoiding the larger ports."

Richard continued, "The freight will be twenty men, not slaves but soldiers, horses, and wagons along with cargo – and that is all you need know. I'm offering one thousand in gold up front, with two thousand more at the time of our safe arrival."

"You got a deal, Mister," said the sailor, with a big smile showing off his diminishing yellow and brown, jagged teeth.

"Colonel," corrected Richard.

"Of course, Colonel, you can call me Captain. Now that we're partners you can remove your hand from that pistol, don't you think?"

Richard had forgotten where his hand lay. "Of course, Captain." He took away his hand and covered the revolver with the flap of his jacket.

The captain pointed to the colonel's waistband. "That's a nice set of Remingtons. You know, I shipped an old man out a' the Carolinas a ways back with guns just the same – what was his name?" The captain was pulling on his whiskers in thought. "Carpathian, that's it, how's he doin'?"

Richard knew this man was dangerous and he would have to keep an eye on him. "He's well, the man is a worthy broker," Richard replied then quickly changed the subject. "Be here tomorrow morning with the sun, the ship will be loaded and ready to sail."

"I'll need a crew, Colonel. Problem is its slim pickins 'round here, the able ones have moved on from this area."

"My men will be at your disposal, Captain."

"I beg your pardon, Colonel, but trainin' soldiers to be sailors takes more time than we got."

"My men can handle it," said Richard. "It's been my experience that Captains carry their own crews, where might your sailors be, sir?"

"I regret they were lost to the sea, a storm took my steamboat. She was not as well-off on the ocean as she was on the lakes and rivers. Not to worry, your vessel here is sound and the weather seems good." The captain turned and headed away down the docks with a wave of his hand, "I'll see you with the sun, Colonel." He faded into the shadows along with the sound of his boot steps, leaving Richard standing alone to wait for the arrival of his men.

◆❖◆

Andelko and the twelve vampires of the coven arrived at the port ahead of the army of men. A blue moon stood straight up in the night sky and lit up a low-lying fog floating just over the ground and stretching out across the top of the water. Richard's attention was immediately drawn to the coven, all newly dressed in western gear taken from the late Adrian Carpathian's storage room. From a distance, they looked like any other hired posse that might travel the west, but up close it became clear they were not human any longer. Andelko met Richard on the boardwalk, leaving the coven lined up on the bank,

"I see you met up with the wagons and the men," stated Richard, as he referred to their dress.

"Yes, you have heard the saying, 'when in Rome'," Andelko replied, with a dramatic wave of his hand. "I believe it will be to our benefit to dress like the Americans when in America."

"There is another saying, my friend; you can dress a pig but underneath it is still a pig."

Andelko put his cold arm around Richard as they walked towards the gang plank. "Richard, I'm concerned about you. You seem to be unsure about our little endeavor."

Richard stopped their movement to face his old friend before he spoke. His main purpose was to escape the grasp upon his shoulder as Andelko's touch actually made his heart ache. "My job has always been to protect you and the coven from vampire assassins and do your daytime bidding. For over a hundred years, I have done so. Leaving the safety of our lands for this new one – let's just say I am having feelings that this could be the beginning of the end."

"You are correct," said Andelko. "There is something going on here that not even I fully understand. But I assure you there is a shift coming in the balance of power, and we will be there to battle for the kingdom of Earth, together."

Richard said nothing in return, he just stepped aside allowing Andelko to walk ahead of him up the gangplank. The twelve vampires of the coven were suddenly behind their master, following him onto the ship. Richard never heard the vampires come from the shore to the dock. When they moved swiftly they were silent, but now that they walked single file up the ramp the sounds they made were like any other person. The sound of their spurred boots and the combination of metal and leather rubbing together from their gunbelts echoed down the boardwalk. The wide brim hats helped conceal their dead looking eyes and their pale, bluish skin; the old dusters they wore made a swishing sound. Their fangs remained hidden as long as the lips remained sealed.

Richard wondered if there were women gunslingers in America, as he could not help noticing the beauty of Elizabeth with her long auburn hair, who smiled and winked at him as she passed. Camellia, Savannah, Anna, and Katrina were all very beautiful as well, they were dark haired of different shades, also flirting with him with winks and provocative tongue gestures as they were the last to board.

Staying behind, Richard suddenly heard the sounds of John Belien and the Army of Twenty as they arrived with the wagons. He felt some relief knowing he would not be alone in the small confines of the ship with the vampires.

The vampires went directly to the sealed quarters down below at the stern of the ship where the whale blubber and oil had once been stored. This area was totally sealed from light, then from mid-ship to the bow was a good area for the holding of the goods and the horses, and the men would remain on deck for the voyage.

The last of the horses were being loaded as the sun was breaking the horizon. Richard watched the captain as he approached down the boardwalk, a duffel bag slung over his shoulder. Richard met the American at the bottom of the ramp and handed him a bag of gold as he stood before him, this was his down payment for the journey.

"I trust the count is correct, Colonel?"

"Count it if you like, Captain. The rest will be yours if we make it to our destination across the sea."

"I have no doubt we will make it," replied the captain. "Only the good die young and my senses tell me there ain't much good aboard this ship."

"Then I am sure you will be quite comfortable aboard our vessel, Captain."

The captain grinned and nodded his head as he walked the gangplank to take his position behind the wheel of the whaling ship. He would sail her back to his homeland, with passengers like none that America had ever seen before.

CHAPTER THIRTEEN

The sword was slung around his right shoulder at his back, the hilt sticking up slightly above his head. The .45 Navy Colts were tied down in their holsters and buckled around his waist. The gunbelt was full of silver bullets in rows all the way around its length. Slung over the left shoulder hung the extra ammo belt, also filled with the cross-cut silver shots. Jack's hat was tethered under his chin in its own battle against the wind while his knee-length duster fought off the swirling sand. He wore tight leather gloves with the thumb and trigger finger cut out for better feel for shooting, and around his neck was a leather scarf. Running his hands along it made him a little uneasy, when he thought about why he would need such protection.

Jack stood at the base of the Black Mountain looking up at a steep trail that led to the top. The climb would be difficult in his boots, except he was no longer wearing boots. He stared at his feet and to his surprise he was wearing lace up Indian moccasins. As he began the climb, the leather shoes had amazing grip on the sand as well as on the rock. Jack made quick work of the trail in his dream, making it to the top as time seemed to stand still. As he pulled himself over the rim, the sky turned black with fast moving clouds and the wind blew steadily.

Jack knew his body was lying on his bedroll in the hogan, while his spirit made this journey to the top of the Black Mesa.

He got to his feet: Standing before him was humanity's enemy, the demon he had confronted in the cave the last time he left his being. Jack walked forward with much conviction, stopping ten feet from the vampire while trying to appear fearless. He wanted to distance himself from the edge of the cliff. Jack was not convinced that his life force would survive such a fall, even though this was not a meeting of the flesh but a spirit meeting through a premonition.

"So," spoke the vampire, "you are the warrior that the Good One has sent. You do realize that you cannot defeat me."

"I might agree," replied Jack, "if this were only a battle of arrogance, you would win hands down."

Andelko was instantly two inches from Jack's face, fangs bared, clearly upset by this insult.

Jack suppressed the panic that was welling within him and stood his ground. He knew it would be a mistake to show fear for this demon to feed upon.

"Back off, bloodsucker," Jack warned. As soon as he spoke the words, a blue light began to radiate through his shirt at his chest. The glowing cross around his neck put the distance of ten feet back between the two as Andelko immediately retreated.

Andelko paced back and forth several times with his hands locked behind his back, appearing to be in deep thought.

Jack's feet were positioned in the same tracks he started in since confronting the vampire at the top of the mountain. He looked calm, but they both could feel his heart pounding.

Andelko stopped pacing and faced Jack before he spoke. "I have decided you may go in peace, gunslinger – ride on far from here, and you will be spared."

"I can't do that, demon. This is my punishment, and I must pay for the sins of my past."

"I see," said Andelko. "You are already at a disadvantage here, for I am being rewarded for the sins of my

past. Maybe you are best suited worshiping the fallen one?"

"I once followed the path of evil," said Jack, as he pulled the leather scarf from around his neck and dropped it to the ground. "But I saw the errors of my ways, and I do repent." He then removed the preacher's collar from his pocket and fastened it around his neck. "I will, one way or the other, be seated beside the Father in Heaven in the end."

The evil laughter that escaped Andelko seemed to come from the bowels of hell as it reverberated across the flat top mountain. The vampire waited until the echoes of his hilarity passed, then threw back the flaps of his coat taking the gunfighter stance; his hands hovered over the butts of his pistols.

Preacher Jack did the same but without hesitation; instinct took over as his duster flew back, he pulled both revolvers, and began firing.

Andelko pulled his pistols and returned fire simultaneously. An explosion of white light flashed, and then they simply vanished. The top of the Black Mesa Mountain was suddenly quiet and still, along with the sky above.

Jack sat up quickly upon his bedroll inside the hogan, and his hands went to his chest, searching for wounds; there were none. He looked across the room for the chief to see empty bedding, he was gone again.

"Great," said Jack aloud, "always sneakin' off somewhere." Rising to his feet, he pushed the hanging blanket aside and walked outdoors. He was glad to see it was early morning, for he now realized that the vampires were restricted to roaming only at night. He had no idea what day it was or what month for that matter; it really did not make a difference any longer.

Jack walked across the encampment toward his wagon, thinking about whiskey the whole way. When he got there, he grabbed the coffee beans instead. A rumbling sound caught his attention; he looked to the mountain to see a storm forming over the top. Instinctively, he reached for his revolvers to find he was unarmed. He found his shotgun in the wagon, loaded it, stuffed his pocket with extra shells, and headed back to the campfire to make coffee.

Where the hell is everybody? he thought as he looked around. The horse line was empty and the place was deserted. *It's like an Indian ghost town around here.*

Jack dropped a handful of coffee beans into the pot and hung it over the fire, leaving it to heat. Then he took the shotgun with him and walked over to where the horses were once tethered. There were hoof prints in the sand where they once stood, but no tracks to show they walked away – it was as if they had just vanished into thin air.

Fires were burning in the hogans, judging from the smoke pouring from the stacks. He knew the chief's was empty, but what about the others? Jack walked the camp and checked each one; they were all empty including the one where the squaws had made the cross-cut bullets of silver.

Jack suddenly realized he had not seen anyone put wood on a fire since he arrived months ago, but there were always fires burning. In fact, there was not a good source of wood here in the desert. *"The bush burned with fire, and the bush was not consumed,"* muttered Jack.

Jack returned to the campfire and poured his coffee, bitter just like he liked it. He looked to the Black Mountain again. Quiet now, because the storm he saw earlier did not form. He retrieved his Good Book from the hogan, seated himself outside by the fire, and began to read in the book of Daniel.

He read aloud: *"The King Darius was forced to cast Daniel into the lion's den, and a stone was brought and laid upon the mouth of the den and sealed with the King's signet. The next morn the King arose and went to the den and cried out to Daniel, O Daniel, servant of the living God, is thy God, whom thou servest continually, able to deliver thee from the lions? Then said Daniel unto the King, 'O King, live forever.' For God had sent his Angel to shut the lion's mouths."*

Jack closed the book and looked around the empty camp; he then glanced up to the sky. "Daniel gits lions and I git vampires," he said with his arms outstretched. "My Lord, why have you forsaken me?" Jack felt irritated and a little depressed as he went back inside his hogan and put the book back into the leather satchel.

He turned to exit when he accidently kicked something with his foot. With a grin, he picked up the half-empty bottle of whiskey and popped the cork, taking a swig as he pushed the cloth door away with the other hand and departed the hogan. To his total shock, he saw the chief from the corner of his eye, seated, and drinking coffee at the fire. He choked a little as he brought the bottle down from his lips; he then looked past to see the horses tied to their tether line with two of the braves brushing them down, seeming like they had been there all along.

Preacher Jack's faith was suddenly reinforced by his thoughts, *Daniel was sent an angel; these Indians must have been sent for me?*

CHAPTER FOURTEEN

The whaling ship's sails were its main propulsion, but it also had two coal-powered steam engines that drove the double paddles. One paddle was positioned on the portside with the other on the starboard side at the stern and off center. The paddles were used for maneuverability when docking and during storms where the waves could reach disastrous size. Eight days into their journey, the weather turned bad for a time, the paddles were deployed as coal was shoveled into the boilers that powered the steam engines by several soldiers of the Twenty. The storm was of medium size, and while extreme, there was no real danger of sinking with the experience of the American captain behind the wheel. The sails were lowered and the paddles were engaged, giving more control to maneuver through the surf. The captain was enjoying himself watching half the land-loving army spew the deck with vomit and hanging on for their lives.

The voyage across the Atlantic would take twelve days or less according to the American, if the weather was good, and if there were no unforeseen problems. Colonel Richard Andersson insisted the captain must put them on the shores of Virginia within ten days, preferably at night, if at all possible.

Richard shadowed the captain at all times, taking turns at the wheel allowing for sleep. When the sky turned dark and the wind picked up the American had taken the wheel and ordered the start of the engines.

By the end of the storm, Richard was green but he refused to heave. He did not want to fuel the joy the captain was having at his men's expense. Instead, he requested a lesson on the wheel with the paddles engaged.

The captain obliged, but with some suspicion. He was not convinced that this warrior from the mountains wanted to learn to steer a ship for his own accomplished curiosity. The American did not trust these foreigners by any means.

The storm had passed and the sails were cast back to their open wind catching position, as they were approximately two days from the shores of the States.

The captain was lying in a low-hanging hammock, giving the impression of sleep, ten feet from Richard who stood at the helm. The captain's thoughts went to the last several days; the soldiers had been taking care of the great Clydesdales that were kept in the cargo hold at the bow of the whaling ship. This hold was open at the top where rope webbing had been woven in three by three squares for containment and stretched across, acting as an open-aired roof. While fighting their seasickness, the men would feed and water the horses and shovel the manure into buckets for throwing over the side into the ocean. The back part of the hold was loaded with crates, saddles, and gear. This was normal procedure for the transporting of men and animals at sea.

What concerned the captain was the holding area at the stern. A set of steps led to the deck below then a double split-steel door in the floor opened to another set of steps leading to the bowels of the ship. This room was where the whale blubber had been stored in the days of fishing operations. Though it had been many years since, there still lingered a slight sent of rotten fish when the doors were opened. The only one who ever went down there was the colonel, and he always had a weary look on his face when he returned. Two soldiers would grab the large handles in the floor and open them, one from each side, the colonel would descend into the pitch-black hold, and the men would close the doors immediately behind him. The strange, dead smell which lingered with the normal stench of old fish that escaped the hold made the captain uncomfortable. He could not figure out what might be down there, but the saying, *curiosity killed the cat,* ran through his mind as he finally drifted into sleep.

"Captain," said Richard, as he smacked the man's boot, "Captain, awake."

He pulled the hat from his face and sat up looking bewildered, "Whaa... What is it?"

"You were mumbling and shuddering," explained Richard. "Nightmare?"

"Yeah, I guess," replied the captain as he wiped the sweat from his brow. "I don't remember nothin'."

"Take the wheel while I break. There's not much wind right now, but those low clouds approaching behind us might change that as we reach the afternoon."

Richard barely finished his sentence before a gust of wind blew up their backside. The large wooden, circular steering wheel began to spin, throwing the ship slightly off course and picking up speed as the sails filled with the breeze.

The captain stood and grabbed the wheel, making the proper adjustments using the compass as his guide. Then he pulled a telescope from a holder fastened to the side of the console and began to scan the distance. He knew they were close to their destination; normally this would excite a sailor, but the captain only felt dismay.

The sun had an hour's time left in the sky before nightfall, when a soldier yelled from the bow of the ship, "Land, I think there's land!" The excitement in his voice could be heard as well as the sounds of every man scrambling to the bow and to the sides of the ship, desperate to see.

These men were soldiers not seamen, and they had been trapped on the ocean for nine days; most had never been on a boat in their lives. If these men were capable of shedding tears, now was the time as the coast of America showed on the horizon.

The captain swung the ship hard to the south, maneuvering it parallel with the shore. Everyone, including the horses, stammered making the ship list to one side, before coming back right.

Richard made his way back to the helm holding on to whatever he could grasp until he made it to the captain's flank.

"What are we doing, Captain?"

"I'm keepin' us afloat, the waters git shallow very quickly on these shores, we must run the coast and find a squash channel."

"How do you know where to find these channels?" asked the colonel.

The captain did not answer at first, but then did so reluctantly. "You see that distant peak there," the captain explained with the point of his finger, "just off the bow to the starboard?"

Richard leaned in and followed the direction of his arm toward the skyline; he was a military man and knew how to read the terrain. "I see the crowning, we drop the sails and use the remaining coal to power our way in, correct?" the colonel asked with some confidence.

"That's the plan," the captain replied. "With this wind it should be around first light."

After a while, Colonel Richard left the American at the wheel and summoned two of his men to the double doors in the floor of the ship as the moon begun to replace the sun in the sky. The moon was bright this night, illuminating everything the color of blue. They would run the coast 'til morning, which would bring them to deeper waters, and then turn inland at the peak toward the Virginia and North Carolina border.

What's down there? wondered the captain as the colonel descended into the deck of the boat, his men quickly closing the doors behind him. *I don't know what it is, but I don't like it,* reeled through the American captain's mind with a slight chill.

The colonel was below in the hull for no more than forty minutes when the doors opened.

And there's that smell again, the smell of death. The captain watched as the soldiers closed the doors and Richard crossed the deck and up the stairs. He expected some kind of order or conversation; instead, he got the barrel of a Remington revolver pointed at his head.

"What the *Hell* is this, Colonel?"

"Captain, I need you to walk down those stairs and enter the hull of the ship through those doors down below."

A fear welled up inside the captain that he did not understand, for he was not afraid of death and he was not scared of any man.

"What for?" he asked.

"You have been wondering what is down there, now is the time."

"You could have just asked, Colonel; the gun is not needed. I thought we were friends?"

"Trust me, the closer you get to that door the more this gun will be necessary. Now let's move."

The captain left the helm and began to descend the stairs that led to the deck. When he did so, a soldier took over the wheel from behind him. The colonel followed, holding his pistol on the man until they reached the front of the double doors, where the two soldiers opened them.

The captain stared down into the darkness. The smell was much stronger down here and every part of his being told him to run, but he would not, for he had never been the type. He looked to his captor and pulled his Navy Colt from his belt, attempting to hand it over to the colonel,

"Keep it," said Richard. "I would not deny a warrior such as you the right to go down fighting."

The captain's confusion showed on his face.

Richard pointed down the stairs with the barrel of the pistol, indicating it was time for him to go.

The captain took two steps downward, but his body suddenly locked up, out of his control. Everything inside him told him not to go down there. His instincts told him to stay and fight for his life up top, against these men. He turned sideways and brought his pistol up toward the colonel. But he was not there, as he had moved around behind the American.

With a boot in the captain's back, Richard pushed him into the pitch-black hull. The soldiers slammed the doors shut then pulled their swords from their sheaths and quickly shoved them through the handles to bar the doors. From inside, gunfire was heard, followed by a blood-curdling scream. The doors banged up and down several times as far as the swords would allow; then there was only silence.

All the soldiers on the ship from bow to stern knew what had just happened. Half the men lowered their heads, giving the sign of the cross with their right hand, brow to chest, left shoulder to right shoulder – the Father, the Son, and the Holy Ghost. Others who had lost their faith long ago just stared off into the distance across the waters, wondering if they might some night suffer the same fate.

Colonel Richard was now the *Captain* of the boat. He ordered his men to drop the sails and fire up the steam engines. Then he turned the ship at the peak that the former captain had shown him and headed for land.

John Belien stood next to his commander and friend as they gazed upon the shoreline of America with anticipation. They managed to forget about the horror down below – at least for a short time.

CHAPTER FIFTEEN

Preacher Jack awoke sitting upright, trying to get his bearings. *Again in this shithole,* he thought, as he looked around the hogan. The chief was at his fire, smoking his pipe. Jack waited for him to speak as he stood and drank water from his canteen. He rubbed his teeth with his finger then swished some around in his mouth before spitting at the ground. He walked to the other side of the room, looking at the old Indian several times, while he washed his face in a cleaning bowl.

"They're here," said Jack. "They're far off, but they have landed on American soil."

"Yes, I feel them," replied White Owl as he exhaled puffy clouds of smoke.

"The Army men who protect the vampires during the day are their slaves, but they are warriors and will fight to the death, as is their duty," Jack stated.

"Yes," replied the chief.

"You know," spoke Jack as he threw his drying rag to the ground with disdain, "you could add a little more to this conversation there, Chief, or any conversation for that matter."

"We must meet the Army of men in the daylight, before they reach the mountain," the chief added.

"Yes," agreed Jack, "we cannot defeat the army and the vampires together. An ambush on the men during the day while the demons sleep might work, but from where?"

Chief White Owl stood. "Come, I will show you," he said, and then he walked outside.

Jack dressed hurriedly; he strapped on his revolvers, grabbed the shotgun, and slung the sword of silver on his back. At the last, he snatched his hat and walked out of the hogan. The chief waited for him on the bare back of his horse. Jack's mount had been saddled and prepared for travel. He noticed a new addition to his arsenal in the saddle scabbard, a Winchester yellow boy rifle.

"Always one step ahead of me ain't yah, Chief?" remarked Jack with a grin.

Jack was not surprised when he did not get an answer or even a comment as the old Injun just turned and rode off toward the sun. Jack mounted his steed and followed.

They rode hard for two hours and then settled in at a walk, the sun was straight up and the sky was clear. Jack knew when they arrived at their destination without being told – the place was perfect for an ambush. The way was ten wagons wide with fifty-foot high canyon walls on both sides, at least a half-mile long, and nothing larger than a desert shrub or cactus to hide behind.

The chief brought them to a halt at the opening of the canyon. He pulled an arrow from his quiver and used it as a pointer while he spoke. "They will come through here, the only pass for many miles. Four braves on top this side, four braves on top on the other with rifles and arrows firing from above, and four braves from behind to drive them to us."

"Us?" asked Jack.

"You and I will confront them here."

"I like it, Chief. I could a' used you in the war," said Jack.

"I have been in many wars." replied White Owl.

"I was referrin' to the Civil War, Chief. Never mind, are we done here? I left the whiskey behind, and I fear my tongue is beginning to swell."

They turned their horses around and rode out of the canyon. A large white owl watched their departure from the top of the cliff before it took flight and followed them from high above, just beyond their distance of sight.

The preacher and the Indian chief followed the same path back to the mountain that brought them to the canyon. They made it about half the distance when Jack noticed the Indian had deviated from the trail. Not knowing if this was purposeful or not, he began to question.

"Uh, Chief, I think we're taking the long way home?"

White Owl said nothing, but continued at a steady pace leading them out of the dry sands toward more moist lands. Trees began to appear, one here and there at first, then more often until they were traveling through forest. Jack's patience was getting thin, he felt like an adolescent being led by his father. With a maneuver off the path and making his own trail, he went around the old Injun and cut him off by stopping his forward progress. Their horses were alongside one another, the emotionless look on the Indian's face irritated Jack further.

"I'm not going one step forward until you tell me where the Hell we're goin'."

The chief raised his arm and pointed down into a ravine. "We go to save your tongue."

Jack looked down into the clearing, a grin forming on his face. "I take it all back, Chief, you're all right."

To Jack's delight, at the bottom of the gorge not more than thirty yards away, smoke billowed out of the stacks of a lean-to with the unmistakable set-up of a still. He could now smell the oak-flavored tequila intertwining with the scent of venison, his mouth began to water. There were three men working around the small camp, and two women – who even from this distance were easy on the eyes. Jack started down the hill and then he stopped his horse when he realized the old Indian was not following. "You are comin' with ain't yah, Chief?"

"I will come for you when the sun rises, for my path this night is not yours."

White Owl moved along the ridge following the trail. Jack watched him then glanced down to the still and when he looked back the chief had vanished. Jack turned his head to the camp down below and was relieved it had not gone missing. It was early afternoon and Jack had not had a drink all day, and the jerky he had this morning was digested long ago.

The three men and two women were very accommodating to Jack's needs for a payment of three American one-dollar gold coins. They got him a deer steak and a gallon jug of Mexican oak-barreled Tequila. The women were extremely friendly, kissing on him from both sides and feeding him bits of meat. The two men made music by fiddle and harp, and created a drinking atmosphere for which Jack was obliged. He danced with the ladies and dropped more coins in the bucket at the musician's feet. He emptied the jug and threw it in the air then blasted it to pieces with one shot of his drawn pistol.

The bootleggers produced another jug for another coin and Jack drank for joy for the first time in years. He finally got to the point where he needed to lay down for a little while. He dropped to the ground, back first, and used the sitting log under his head for a pillow. The girls sat on each side of him and began to massage his hands. Jack felt peaceful and relaxed as he drifted off. The last thing he remembered was a sight in the darkening sky of the biggest, indigo-colored, full moon he had ever seen.

Jack was deep in a drunken sleep from the moonshine from his newly found friends who lived in this strange forest in the middle of the desert. He had not slept this deeply in years, and he allowed his guard to drop more than anyone in this time or place should. His quiet bliss began to erode as he began to dream, slowly bringing him back to consciousness.

White Owl's old leather face gradually appeared into his mind, "Awake, Preacher, awake."

"It's not mornin', Chief. Can't you leave me be just this once?"

"Evil is upon you, Preacher," warned White Owl. "The test is real, the fallen one must not keep you from reaching the Black Mountain. Now open your eyes!"

Jack's eyes snapped open. In a split second, he saw the two naked women change from their human form to hairy beasts, standing upright as their noses turned to teeth-filled snouts, and their eyes became those of an animal with fur the color of the moon. Jack did not wait for their claws to reach their full length. He slid underneath the creatures as they lunged for his throat where his head once rested against the log.

He scrambled to his feet and turned, at the same time pulling his revolver and slamming the hammer down with the palm of his left hand. They had turned also and two bullets of silver hit the left protruding breast of the beast to his right, knocking her back and over the log. The wolf bitch to his left was surprisingly fast as she sprang off her hindquarters with a growling rage,

Jack fell to his back, but managed to bend his legs and stick his boots just below her ribcage. With everything he had, he pushed his legs out straight, knocking the beast backwards. Jack created enough distance to quickly fire, thumbing the hammer first and then pulling the trigger with his index finger – *click, bang; click, bang; click, bang.* The first bullet shattered the beast's bottom jaw completely off, the next vanished through the hole and out the back of the head, and the last removed the left eye.

Without hesitation, Jack jumped to his feet as he sensed a rush from his left. He turned and fired as the wolf-man knocked him off his feet; the Remington pistol hit the forest floor as he could not keep it in his grasp. The creature shot past him then turned on all fours, slowly, growling deep from within. Jack had managed to roll to his feet as he reached for his second revolver to find his holster empty. As his eyes wildly searched the ground, two more of the male beasts approached from the woods surrounding him.

They had him in the center of a triangle, each one pacing and growling. He moved with them as they slowly circled, until he almost tripped backward over the very log he once slept upon. From the corner of his eye, Jack spotted the hilt of his sword leaning against the downed timber. He took the two steps and pulled the sword of silver from its sheath with both hands then raised it over his head in a warrior's high stance.

The man-wolves let out a howl, one after the other, that echoed through the forest, and then they attacked, one, two, and three, from left to right. The preacher warrior swung the sword, leveling it with the neck of one of the up-right wolves and separated the head from its body. A flash of blue light ran down the weapon on contact all the way to the preacher's elbows before extinguishing. He continued the swing, all in one motion spinning and dropping to one knee while taking off the legs at mid-thigh of the second charging beast. The blue flashed to his elbows then faded as the third leaped at him with teeth bared.

Jack thrust the sword forward through the gut and up to the hilt. The weight of the demon creature was great and Jack was forced to use all his strength to keep the snapping jaws mere inches from his face from ripping him to pieces. This time the blue fire began with the cross that lay upon Jack's chest, went up his arms, and traveled up the sword. With a flash that lit up the trees close to their tops, it seared his attacker.

Jack rolled the smoldering body of the wolf-man to the side and off him to the forest floor.

There was nothing but quiet as Jack lay there for a moment, breathing hard and listening intently for any movement. Slowly the sounds of the woods returned – crickets, frogs, and the buzz of the insects. Jack got to his feet and, with sword in hand, he began to collect his guns scattered about. He reloaded the empty cylinders of the one pistol then found the loaded one he had lost and slid it back into its holster. The woods became silent once again.

Jack heard a groan from behind him; he spun quickly, wielding the sword, and then walked over to the source of the noise. The moonshiner had reverted to his human shape, but with his legs missing. Jack looked to the dark sky; the clouds had rolled in and blanketed the moon. As they cleared out, the moon began to shine once again. The man started to change back to his wolf form.

Without delay, Jack took the point of his sword and pressed it to the temple of the being. "Back to Hell, demon," he said as he speared it through the head and into the ground. He was forced to squint at the bright flash of blue light. The preacher pulled his cross from under his shirt and kissed it as he thanked the Lord for his strength of spirit. The chatter of insects and the night sounds of the forest returned to normal.

Jack prepared for travel, relieved that his horse was spared, and had been tied well enough not to flee. He dragged the bodies into the lean-to and piled them up; in death, they had all gone back to human form. Jack had to remind himself what they had once been to justify in his mind his role in their death. He removed the Good Book from his saddlebag and said a prayer over the fallen.

PSALM 3: 1 – 8, LORD, how are they increased that trouble me! Many are they that rise up against me. Many there be which say of my soul, there is no help for him in God, Selah. But thou, O LORD art a shield for me; my glory, and the lifter up of mine head. I cried unto the LORD with my voice, and he heard me out of his holy hill. Selah. I laid me down and slept; I awakened; for the LORD sustained me. I will not be afraid of ten thousands of people, that have set themselves against me round about. Arise, O LORD; save me, O my God; for thou has smitten all mine enemies upon the cheek bone; thou hast broken the teeth of the ungodly. Salvation belongeth unto the LORD; thy blessing is upon thy people. Selah.

Jack closed the book, went to his log, and sat upon it to wait for sunrise and the arrival of the chief.

Jack didn't pray and didn't think. He rested his body and mind with a blankness of total bliss that rejuvenated him to the total abilities of his strength. With his eyes locked open in a stare, he finally blinked with the coming of the morn. The preacher looked up and to his right to see the chief sitting upon his horse on the ridge. He got to his feet and mounted his horse; swatting the reins to the hindquarters to push the animal up the steep hill. He did not stop until they reached the top and he was face to face with the old Injun warrior.

"Where the Hell have you been there, Chief?"

"I had my own demons to face. I see your sword found you worthy."

"Yeah," said Jack, clear irritation in his voice, "no thanks to you. You know, I'm gittin' a little old for this cloak and dagger shit."

"Once the top of the mountain is reached and the battle begins, you will not have much time to question." said White Owl. Without waiting for a reply, he turned his horse and walked it away along the path at the top of the ravine.

Jack lit a cigar as he watched the chief from behind, took a long draw and inhaled deeply, then clutched it between his teeth. He slid the rifle from the scabbard, cocked it, and aimed at the barrel of shine and pulled the trigger. The bullet pierced the still, igniting it with a flash of fire, catching the lean-to and the bodies inside. Preacher Jack put the rifle away.

"The serpents have been cast out from this Garden of Eden and cast down into the Hell fire," said Jack as he followed White Owl's path without looking back.

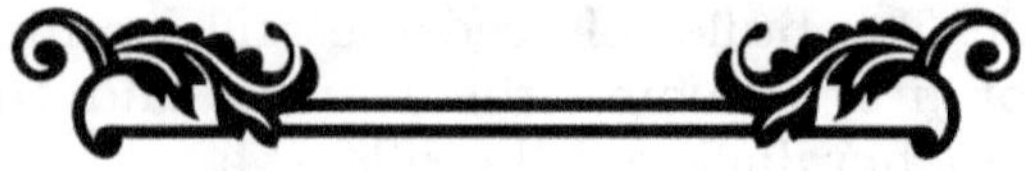

CHAPTER SIXTEEN

Colonel Richard Andersson, Captain John Belien, and the Army of Twenty docked the whaling ship in a port on the border of Virginia and North Carolina two hours before sundown. The docks were well hidden and not sanctioned by the port authority. The settlement was made up of three buildings run by men of questionable integrity. There were larger ports to the north and the south, but this one the pirates and scoundrels of the sea preferred, as cash was king and the only regulations were the amount one must pay. The illegal slave trade and the banned drug from the east called Opium regularly ran through there. The men that managed the docks were the lowest of the low; they did not care for God or country, they only cared about their own wealth. But even they could feel something was not quite right about this ship, its men, and the cargo from the minute it reached port.

Five well-armed men greeted the ship as it docked, realizing immediately they were outnumbered and outgunned. Some thought they were witnessing the docking of a ghost ship as the foreign army, such as they had never seen, stepped seemingly out of the past. Their fears and concerns were quickly set aside and replaced by their greed when Richard ordered two soldiers to place an iron box onto the dock; the top was opened to reveal it full of Roman gold coins. The Devil himself could be on that ship, which was not far from the truth, as far as the keepers of the port were concerned; their price had been met.

They were told by Captain John Belien to retire to their shelters with their payment from the time of the setting of the sun 'til the break of day. The ship would also be theirs to do with what they would after the army had moved on.

The great Clydesdales were walked off the ship first, to graze on the shores and get their land legs back under them after the long and unstable days at sea. The wagons were difficult to unload for they were wider than the dock's walkway. After removing the cargo, the soldiers had to carry them to land one at a time, and by the third wagon, their legs and bodies were attuned to the steady ground.

Finally, the Army was prepared for travel, awaiting orders from the colonel who had yet to join them from the lower deck of the ship.

John Belien was on his horse holding onto the reins of the colonel's mount waiting for his return. He was nervous as always whenever Richard met with the vampires. If they devoured or turned Richard, then John would be in charge and would have to deal with the vampires directly – that he did not want. John felt relief when he saw Richard walking toward him, down the gangplank of the ship.

Richard and John went over the maps of this strange land, deciding the best route. They would head south, close to the coast through North Carolina, South Carolina, then through Georgia, and the Florida panhandle. This was not the most direct route, but it would avoid mountains and thick forests.

Andelko and the coven would travel a different path, under the cover of night, straight through the mountains, dependent on caves and mineshafts to protect them from the daylight.

John put his maps away as he and the colonel moved their men out. They would ride during the night and the day, only resting in the early morn for three hours in every twenty-four. The wagons were resupplied with food, beer, water, and liquor from the port keepers who were more than happy to give up their stocks for the box of gold that made every man there rich beyond their dreams.

The coffins were left on the ship to make room for supplies. Andelko was confident they were no longer needed. If the coven could not find proper shelter, they could burrow into loose earth and use the ground for their protection.

The Army would hunt along the way whenever they came across the tracks of deer, bear, or any other large meaty animals. The vampires would hunt as well, but they would most likely hunt humans; may God bless their souls.

Colonel Richard, John Belien, and the Army of Twenty were two hours gone; all seven of the men of the port were locked in the very large saloon and eatery as instructed on the conditions for their payment of the gold coin filled box. They drank and ate and carried on talking of the directions and places they would go with the rising of the sun, using their newfound wealth. The iron box of Roman coins was open on a wood table, the leader of this rabble was preparing to split up the loot as he deemed fair, when the latched wooden door blasted open.

The men drew their weapons and aimed toward the open doorway. At first, there was nothing but the sound of wind blowing, and only the outside darkness could be seen; until Andelko entered, along with the coven.

The vampires lined up behind Andelko, six on one side and six on the other. The hissing sound when they bared their fangs was all the men needed to begin firing their pistols and shotguns in terror. The bullets hit their targets but passed through the bloodsuckers' bodies, leaving no permanent wounds.

The fangslingers pulled their pistols and fired, the sound deafening as the room quickly filled with smoke. The weapons of the men were useless as the undead predators dropped their empty guns and lunged, viciously tearing them to pieces and draining every bit of their warm blood from their leaking bullet wounds. In minutes it was over, the shrunken dehydrated bodies were strewn about in an unidentifiable mess. The gunfight was not necessary, but ordered by Andelko for the playing of his little game. The coven rather enjoyed it, anything was better than being confined to the Drazon Castle of their homeland. They were just pleased to be feeding on humans as was their purpose in this world.

The vampires left the shores, heading inland toward the mountains with unheard of speed, but not before General Barrick scooped up the iron box of gold, carrying it effortlessly, regardless of its great weight.

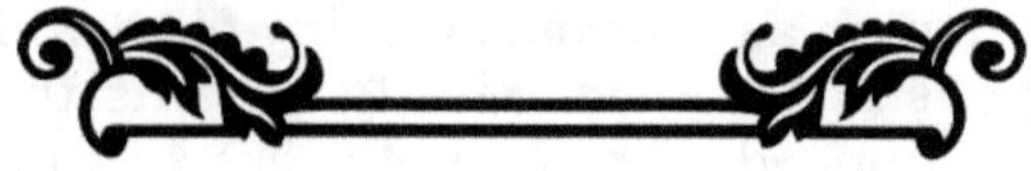

CHAPTER SEVENTEEN

White Owl and the preacher left the woods behind for the open sands of the desert and found their way back to the path that led to their camp at the base of the mountain. Neither man had said a word since they left the forest with the chief not giving up information and Jack tired of trying to drag it out of him.

They reached higher ground after several hours of travel. Jack stopped and drank water from his canteen and then filled his palm several times to wash his face. He turned his head and looked back toward the garden for the first time. A giant cloud of smoke bloomed into the sky above it; the woodlands around the still had caught fire and by tomorrow morn, there would be nothing left but burnt out ruins. Jack knew it wasn't a dream, the proof was clear to see for many miles. *Good riddance,* thought Jack, *to an evil garden masked by beauty that won't trap travelers any longer.* He grabbed a large piece of jerky from his saddlebag, stuck it between his teeth, and kicked his horse into a gallop to catch up with White Owl.

Jack rode alongside the old Indian for a time, waiting patiently for him to speak. As usual, Jack would have to start the conversation. If this old Injun was teaching him anything, it was surely patience.

"Hey Chief, the ambush in the ravine is a solid idea, but there's one problem," Jack gave White Owl time to respond, but he did not so he rolled his eyes and continued, "How will we know when the Army will pass through there? We might have to hole up there for days or weeks to catch 'em."

"The braves are riding to shadow the Army, they will follow them and observe. When the white men are two days from the canyon, they will send word and meet us at the ravine."

"That's good, Chief; you think you could have told me this to ease my mind?"

"I just spoke of this, were you not listening?" the chief said plainly.

Jack laughed a little, looking for an expression on the Indian's face. "If I didn't know better, Chief, I'd say you were joshin' me?"

"I don't know this, Josh," White Owl said seriously.

Jack busted out laughing.

White Owl gave Jack a look that read, *You're a babbling idiot*, which made Jack hoot even harder, his neck stretched back in laughter. When Jack opened his eyes to a clouding sky, he spotted the wingspan of the owl, which silenced him. High in the sky and heading in a straight line for what Jack thought would be the direction the foreign Army would approach from. The owl was white and larger than most, taking flight in the hours of the day, unusual for a creature that hunted at night. Jack watched the great bird flying toward a ridge of mountains. *It would take me a week to git there*, thought Jack, *and he'll be there – Hell, he's there already.* Jack did not totally understand what role the owl played in all this but he could feel the good radiating from this creature.

White Owl and Preacher Jack rode the trail back to their camp located at the base of the Black Mesa Mountain without any trouble. There was nothing left to do but wait for the braves to return with news of the location of the foreign army. Jack had no desire to kill these men, but they were the daytime protectors of the vampires, so they must be considered enemies. Once fighters of men with honor, they were now warriors enslaved by the undead; they were an *Army of the Damned.*

Jack somehow knew all this from the premonitions in his dreams and he would have no problem engaging these men in battle and killing them. They were all faceless warriors to Jack, except for the leader. This one's features were clear and almost recognizable. Jack did not understand how he could know of this man. He knew he was from a different time and place, he knew he was infected with evil, but not totally damned – not yet. Preacher Jack would pray for him, and knew he must face the colonel at some point, to either kill him or save him, it was not clear which. Jack thought to ask the chief about this and then decided against it; sometimes a man must bear his burdens alone.

White Owl sat with his legs crossed in front of the hogan fire and had stared straight ahead for days now, without expression.

Jack's thoughts made him weary; the hogan seemed to be getting smaller and smaller around him. He could not understand how the old Injun could sit there for this long of a time and do nothing but smoke his pipe on occasion. Jack stood after eating a small meal, and spoke up, unable to stand the silence any longer; "Hey Chief, are you sure you aren't kin to Sitting Bull?"

The question broke the Indian's stare, his eyes met Jack's for a moment, but he said nothing. He relit his foot-long pipe and puffed away in silence.

Jack scoffed with a headshake and left the confines of the lodge, grabbing his sword as he pushed the hanging blanket out of his way. He slung the blade over his shoulder by the strap at his back and headed straight for the wagon. "Damn Injuns, got no sense of humor," complained Jack as he reached the wagon. He pulled a bottle of whiskey from the back end of the cart and popped the cork then tipped the bottle back and took a long draw.

He heard thunder off in the distance. Jack looked to the top of the mountain to see black clouds forming. He took another gulp, smacked the cork back into the bottle, and returned it to the box. He then lit a cigar and with it hanging from his lips, he pulled the sword over his head from its sheath and began to practice his swordplay. A soldier, who had turned preacher only to lose his faith, now he was a preacher and a warrior of good. From the high stance, he swung his blade from straight up to left then to right. He spun, and with a level swing he slashed and thrust through the air with great speed and discipline. The preacher's mind was clear for the first time in days, thinking of nothing but his preparation, and passing time for the sake of his sanity.

◆❖◆

Colonel Richard Andersson, Captain John Belien, and the Army of Twenty had been traveling all day and most of the night for over two weeks now. They had made their way through North Carolina, South Carolina, Georgia, then along the straight borderline of the Florida Panhandle that seemed to invade the south end of Alabama. They were now traveling along a new border, dead center between Jackson, Mississippi, and Baton Rouge, Louisiana, when one of the men rode up from the rear to the front of the line where the colonel and the captain led.

Colonel, Captain," said the regular from his saddle.

"What is it soldier?" asked Captain John.

"I could not be certain at first, but I am sure of it now; we are being followed."

"How long soldier?"

"I sensed it forty miles ago, and then I began seeing shadows deep in the forest on both sides. If it had been in the hours of darkness I would of thought it was the...you know...the *fangers*."

The captain spoke up, "They are called Lords to you, soldier, nothing else."

"Yes sir, Captain."

"Never mind that," interrupted Colonel Richard. "Continue on, soldier."

"Sir, I caught sight of what I believe they call the Red Man."

"You saw an American Indian?" asked the captain skeptically.

"Yes sir, I have seen drawings," the soldier replied.

"What exactly did you see?" asked Colonel Richard.

"I just got a glimpse and then he vanished into the brush. He was tan in color, had feathers on his head, was barely clothed, and riding on a lean barebacked horse, sir."

"All right, soldier," ordered the colonel. "Quietly alert the men and keep your eyes watchful, make no moves unless attacked or ordered."

"Yes sir, Colonel." The soldier turned the great horse around, telling the men to be on their guard until further notice as he made his way back to his position in the ranks.

"What do you think, John?" Richard asked.

"I have had the feeling of being watched for the last fifty miles, short of seeing any movement."

"Take the lead, Captain," spoke Richard. "When we reach that clearing up ahead, I am going to fall back to the rear and see what I can see. Whatever arises, take no action, just keep the men moving forward."

"You're the boss," John replied, "but do not get yourself killed. The last thing I want to be is the consular to the vampires."

Richard turned the Clydesdale out of line when they reached the clearing in the woods. Someone had forested the timber here some time ago, as there were cut stumps scattered for acres. There were twelve-foot high pine saplings growing throughout the area, but these woodlands were much thinner than the trail where they had been traveling.

Richard came alongside the soldier who had come forward earlier; he had taken his rightful place in line at the rear of the Army of Twenty. The soldier nodded his head slightly to their right, but did not speak. Richard scanned in that direction.

Amazed, he saw an American Indian keeping pace with them off in the distance, weaving through the thicker brush. He then saw another, farther off, and a little ahead of the first. They were tan-colored, wearing nothing but leather flaps around their waist. They carried bows and a quiver of arrows slung over their shoulders, the other hand held a rope that was bridled around the horse's muzzle.

Colonel Richard left the ranks and maneuvered the big horse in a straight line through the saplings and knee-high brush directly toward the warriors. He reached five horse lengths from the Indians before they quickly rode off through the thicket, Richard tried to follow, but their smaller animals were swifter and the distance between them grew. Richard brought his horse to a stop and watched them flee. The woods they were headed for were as thick as a wall.

There's nowhere to go, thought Richard. He smugly watched, expecting the red men to slow down and turn, but they did not. They were going to crash their animals into the vine-covered foliage that would surely entangle them, forcing a halt. Richard waited in anticipation for the collision. His eyes widened in disbelief as he watched the Indians and their horses go right through the barrier of greenery; they simply vanished into thin air. The branches and leaves shimmered slightly, but did not open to make an entryway. *There are unknown forces in this land, just like in my own,* ran across Richard's mind. He did not sense that these Indians were evil, and Richard knew true evil. This meant these forces might be set against him and his Army, since they fought for the vampires. Richard left the thicket and rode to catch up with his men, feeling a state of wonder inside for what he had witnessed.

Richard made his way back. His men had been on total alert, but eased up when they saw it was their commander. He approached them from off their flank and rode past. The thuds of the great horses' hooves and the sounds of their heavy breaths reverberated through their nostrils, the rubbing leather and clanking of the steel echoed through the woods for long distances, and Richard was reminded that this army was not sneaking up on anyone. The Indians were silent and only seen because they allowed it.

The trail was wide, allowing the colonel to ride alongside his captain at the front of the group.

"You look fit. Did you slay them all with one swipe of your sword?" said the captain, sarcasm in his voice.

Richard ignored his mockery. "They are not here for battle or they would not have allowed us to have seen them until their attack was upon us."

"We must be traveling on their land," said the captain. "I can imagine that the sight of our Army would bring distress to any primitives."

"Do not underestimate these Indian warriors, Captain. I suspect they came from where we are heading, a scouting party to monitor our progress. They are being driven by an unknown force; a force I believe will go against the vampires."

John looked to his colonel, "That means they will go against this Army. These men are the best warriors of their time, the best that Europe has to offer – we will crush them, as is our purpose," boasted Captain John Belien.

"Your pride is honorable, John, but like the vampires, it is sometimes hard to kill what is already dead."

John did not quite catch the true meaning of his friend and commander's words for his attention was diverted to the woods. He spotted movement off to his left over the shoulder of his colonel. "Our shadow has returned to our flanks, off to your left."

Richard did not turn his head to look, there was no need. "They are on our right flank as well."

The captain glanced to his right to see the Indians off in the distance beyond the clearing. They somehow kept pace with the army even though they had to maneuver constantly through the thicker woods. John now realized Richard's meaning. Their silent movement almost seemed ghostly. It was suddenly revealed to his mind, starting from his gut and working its way upward, that where he was headed could possibly be the end of his time on this Earth, his last battle in a war for humanity.

◆❖◆

Andelko Balas and the twelve vampires of the coven traveled from dusk until dawn, taking refuge during the daylight hours in deep caves in the mountains, and twice burying themselves in the loose earth. The vampires fed upon cattle, horses, and deer for most of their journey. They took human life several times as they came across families trying to survive on their small farms. The coven would eat the women and children, draining them dry. Andelko would insist the men face him in a gunfight, Wild Bill Hickok style. The master vampire never missed; the men did their best, some hitting the vampire, but the lead from their bullets had little effect.

General Barrick thought this cowboy shit a waste of time, referring to it as *the Master playing with his food again.* He never mentioned this to Andelko's face, but he knew his master somehow read his mind whenever he pleased. He could not help his thoughts anymore than he could control his lust for blood. He was the general of this coven and would run it his way, unless overruled by his maker, of course.

The vampires kept pace with the Army of Twenty. They could have passed them and left them behind, easily reaching their destination, but Andelkos orders given due to his premonitions would not allow it. Andelko's master, the one that devoured his parents and turned him long ago, came to him during his daytime rest. He still did not know his name, but he did show him visions of the Black Mountain and the great battle against the Preacher of Good. They were only glimpses, and the end was not revealed. In his arrogance, Andelko had no doubt he would be victorious and evil would rule the earth for a thousand years, earlier than was written.

As time passed, Richard and his Army became expendable and had already come close to serving their purpose, so Andelko was told by his visions. The thought of Richard, his oldest and dearest friend, being sacrificed was troublesome to him, but he could not resist his place by the fallen one's side. The Army of Twenty would be left to fend for themselves, following their own path as Andelko and his coven would move on toward the Black Mesa, leaving the human army behind as a decoy to possibly kill the Preacher and keep him from reaching the mountain.

Andelko was disturbed by his new orders, but he would follow them as his premonitions told.

CHAPTER EIGHTEEN

Weeks passed, Jack did not know how many. His visions decreased, allowing him to get his much needed rest. He slept day and night as his body required, in between prayer and swordplay.

Two of the braves did not ride out in search of the European Army, but stayed behind in the camp. Jack rode along with them on several hunts in the valley and helped them with the killing of three mule deer. The Navajo squaws made quick work of the gutting and skinning of the does on their return and carved most of the meat for drying. Jack filled his saddlebags with the jerky strips. When the time came for his journey to the ravine, he would need quick nourishment in battle.

Jack was not convinced that their ambush would work against the day riders. First of all, the army must travel through the canyon, but any commander worth his grain of sand would realize the dangers of this path. Second, when would they arrive? The chief and his warriors, along with Jack, would have to be in place on the ridges of the gorge well before they entered to catch them in the middle between entry and exit. The large animals would ride nose to tail; with their numbers, it would require the timing of the attack to be precise to catch them between the rock walls with nowhere to go. If any escaped the narrow ravine, they would have to be chased down and confronted in the open desert. The Europeans' horses were massive and strong, but the smaller ponies the Indians rode were faster and more maneuverable. The soldiers had an advantage at hand-to-hand combat; they had guns, swords, and years of battle skill. How they would match up with the Indians was unclear.

Preacher Jack suspected that the chief and his braves were ghosts or maybe angels; he wasn't sure which, maybe both? He was fairly sure the army from the east were men, not spirits; but they were here to protect the worst evil this world had seen since the serpent infiltrated the Garden of Eden.

Jack was running out of patience; he had been fully dressed and geared up for many days, waiting to move this battle forward. He had finished preparing his horse and began walking toward the hogan to confront White Owl and demand he tell him all that he knew when he heard the sounds of the horses gallop. He turned to see White Owl pass by him to meet his brave. They spoke briefly in their native tongue then the chief spoke to Jack,

"The white army is coming, and they travel the canyon road."

Jack's eagerness quickly turned to dread as he realized this was really going to happen. "Well, it's about time," he replied in his most convincing voice. Jack felt concern at the fact that he was going against the army of men and not the evil he must face later. They could lose this battle, or be depleted? He wanted as many warriors as possible available when the time came to face the vampires.

White Owl led the way with Jack and the braves riding hard as they headed for the pass where the first battle would take place. As the dust kicked up behind the horses' fast moving Brng hooves, Jack looked to see the outlined wingspan of a great bird flying high out in front of them, soaring in the direction of the canyon.

♦ ❖ ♦

White Owl, Jack, and the braves reached the ravine within two clicks of the sun. They steered their horses up the backside of the rocky slope to the top of the fifty-foot high cliff where the Navajo warriors were lined up, lying in wait. Jack and the chief stopped at the end of the canyon, just above where they would confront any soldiers who made it through the shower of arrows. Jack could see the Injuns spread out across both sides of the cliff. Bows in hand, they had many arrows stuck in the ground in a line in front of them, set up for easy access to reload and aim, then loose. They would catch the army in the ravine with nowhere to go but forward. With arrows firing at ground level from behind and overhead, the ambush had the potential to become a slaughter.

White Owl left Jack and rode the line to have words with his braves, but soon returned to where Jack smoked his cigar from the back of his horse. He came alongside the preacher and stared forward across the canyon; he did not speak. Jack seemed to read his thoughts, and what he sensed coming from the old Injun was a confidence he wished he could tap into.

"I don't know, Chief," said Jack. "Is this too easy?"

White Owl said nothing; he was a great listener, but his conversing skills needed some work.

"I can't imagine that any military man would bring his army through here; it's suicide," explained Jack with some doubt.

"Your Book of Good talks of many sacrifices," spoke the chief. "The soldiers are merely men; the fallen one uses them for his will."

"As God uses us for His," replied the Preacher. "I am just a man, you and your braves; well, I don't rightly know what you are. Will you also be sacrificed?"

"We already have," White Owl replied."

The chief turned with no more to say on any subject, and led the preacher down the mountainous cliff to the end of the ravine where they would confront any soldiers who made it through the barrage of arrows from above. The soldiers would have two choices. They could withdraw to where they entered the gorge and run into four armed Injuns at the rear. Or they could move forward toward the opening at their front, where White Owl and Jack lay in wait.

Jack suspected that the seasoned warriors would fight to the death, his or theirs.

◆❖◆

Colonel Richard and his Army moved efficiently through the strange lands. The maps they possessed were accurate and Captain John Belien's expertise reading them was sound. They had traveled for many days without the shadow of the Indians at their flanks; they had vanished as quickly as they had appeared.

The Army of Twenty was now the Army of Seventeen. They had lost two soldiers crossing Texas and one died in New Mexico, just outside the Northern Arizona border. All three of the soldier's deaths were of natural causes. Not one of the living spoke of it, but they figured the three men got off easy – for death was the only discharge out of this army, and a natural death was the most peaceful.

The open sands the army had been traveling for many days eventually led them to a landscape of mountainous terrain. It was mid-afternoon and very hot, the line of horses and wagons were brought to a halt at the opening of a gorge that appeared to cut through the mountains.

Captain John shouted out orders to the men, "One hour! Half rations of water and grain for the horses, the beer and rum will remain sealed until further notice, water only."

The soldiers dismounted, pulled the water barrels from the wagons, then filled the troughs, and lined up the massive horses for watering. The horses were always taken care of first, followed by the men from the bottom to the top as is the chain of command.

Colonel Richard and Captain John wiped sweat from their brows as they assessed the area, looking to the cliffs and the narrow passage through them.

"We must go around the mountains, Colonel. The narrow ravine is undefensible." The captain warned before drawing water from his canteen.

"It would take three, four days, John, maybe longer. The provisions are running low and we don't even know if there is a water source on the other side of this God forsaken wasteland."

"If there are any warriors in this land, men or spirits that would dare attack this army, this place is where they will do it. Colonel, I feel a presence here."

Richard dismounted; John did the same. He then came around the large horse to face his colonel. Richard put his hands on the shoulders of his second in command, as a friend more than as his commander.

"I know, John, I feel it too, but we have our orders. Every bit of my military training screams out at me not to lead my men down that road. You know the maps better than I." Richard released John and raised his arm, pointing down the path between the cliffs, "and the way to water is most likely through there."

Captain John shook his head in defeat; he knew they must go through, even though it could mean their death. "Yes, you are right, but I ask of you one request?"

Richard nodded in agreement.

"When I die, do not bury me in this strange land like the others. Instead, burn my body allowing the winds to carry my soul across the sea to the country of my birth."

"You have my word," said Richard, with a grin rarely seen. "Give the men an extra hour then we move out."

The captain left Richard to ponder their situation as he went to check on the men and relay their orders. John was satisfied his friend and commander would grant his request at any cost.

The men of the seventeen were refreshed and prepared for battle, each soldier knowing the potential trap they were about to enter. They also knew they would rather die in battle than dwindle away in the desert of starvation and dehydration. The six horses that pulled the wagons would surely die in the desert, so were shot as they left the wagons behind. Every man carried a portion of the dwindling provisions.

The last great warriors from the east followed single file atop the massive Clydesdales. Their commander led them down the path; all were ordered to be as quiet as possible. The only sounds were the rubbing and clanking of leather against steel, mingled with horse hooves and snorts. The tension built slowly, the farther they got inside the walls of the canyon, the more vulnerable their position became. They looked to the top of the cliffs, knowing any attack would come from there; the term *'sitting duck'* ran across the minds of each and every one of them.

The Army reached the center between the entrance and the exit of the ravine and the fifty-foot walls loomed straight up on both sides, leaving them without options. Richard had the strange feeling this canyon was specifically built for the purpose of ambushing him and his Army. If so, this conflict was much bigger than he and his men, they would be pawns in a battle on a game board being played by the powers to be.

Colonel Richard suddenly heard an echoing screech from above; he raised a closed fist, giving the signal for the Army to halt. He looked to the sky to see a great white bird circling overhead. He then saw the Indians as they appeared at the edge of the cliffs, their bows in hand and arrows loaded. They appeared to be the same kind of natives who had shadowed them in the woods, many miles and many days from here.

"Shields!" ordered Captain John with a yell back to the ranks.

The men pulled their shields from their hanging positions on the saddles and brought them overhead, just as the Indians loosed their arrows upon them. Three soldiers went down immediately, the arrows piercing down through their necks and backs, four were wounded – hit in the legs, arms, and one in the lower buttocks.

"Soldiers at the rear – Retreat!" the colonel yelled out. "Soldiers at the front – Charge!" Richard immediately knew he had made a fatal mistake entering the gorge and there was nothing to do but try to get them out of there as quickly as possible.

The arrows continued to rain down as the forces split, half rode back the way they had come even as the colonel and the front men rode forward. There was nowhere else to go; it was a turkey shoot like none these seasoned warriors had ever seen before.

The soldiers at the rear were picked off one by one; only three made it past the point where the Indians were positioned above. The Clydesdales thundered toward the entrance of the gorge, the three soldiers could taste their freedom – not only the freedom from death by the Indians' arrows – but freedom from the vampires that enslaved them. They would ride until they could ride no more and take their chances in a strange desert land far from home. The three soldiers never saw the braves at their front and to the side positioned at the ground level; they fell from the backs of their horses, dead before they hit the ground, bodies riddled with arrows piercing their sternums and stopping their hearts.

The colonel and the captain led the front half of the men forward toward the opening. As soon as they were out of range of the arrows, the colonel slowed to a halt. He sensed another trap, and he sensed *someone*? There was room now for John to come alongside him and then they turned toward the men. Three empty horses ran past; only two regulars had made it.

Captain John Belien looked into the ravine to find dead horses and dead soldiers scattered as far as he could see. John evaluated the two men who made it through, one had an arrow in his thigh which he twisted and pulled out with a growling yell. The other had one in his back, too deep to remove without some sort of surgery.

"How bad is it, Soldier?" asked the captain.

"I'm done," replied the regular, gasping for breath. "It's in my kidney. Don't let them take me, sir."

"No worries, Soldier. I will not allow the savages to get at your scalp."

The regular looked straight at the captain with pleading eyes. "I refer to the vampires, sir. If I am still living when the night comes, I request an honorable death."

John nodded in agreement and turned to see that Richard had made his way farther up the ravine toward the opening. He seemed to be staring forward at nothing John could see. John scanned the top of the cliffs before riding up to his colonel's side.

"The Army is wiped out, like I warned. I don't know if any of the men made it out the back—"

"None made it out," said Richard, interrupting the captain in mid-sentence.

John heard a thud from behind, he looked back to see the soldier he had just spoken with lying on the ground motionless, the other dismounted and put his fingers to his neck. The regular turned toward the captain and shook his head side to side, and then gave the sign of the cross before closing the dead man's eyes.

"What are we going to do now, Richard?" demanded John. "It will be dark in three hours and I don't want to be anywhere around here when those vampires discover we led their army into an ambush."

"Where are you going to go, John?" Richard replied, and then continued without allowing his friend to answer, "You know there is nowhere to hide from Andelko. Besides, the outcome of this battle has not been decided just yet."

The colonel moved his horse forward at a walk. Then John spotted what Richard had seen at the top of the ridge that led out of the ravine. Two men, one an old Indian with a large feathered head covering and the other a cowboy wielding a great sword, were on horseback. Apparently, they waited to confront any survivors who made it this far out of the gorge.

Richard continued advancing upward toward the flat, drawn to the white man on horseback. As he approached, they turned and rode at a walk out of sight clearing the road. John Belien and the regular came alongside the colonel. When the old Indian and the cowboy vanished over the ridge, a line of Indian warriors appeared at the top of the crest, looking down upon them. They pulled back their bows and let loose their arrows. The captain and the regular fired their rifles several times in desperation before falling dead to the desert ground with many arrows protruding from their bodies.

Three arrows were fired at Richard and with great speed he pulled his sword from its sheath. The blade cut the arrows in half out of midair. He slid off his horse, and debated using the Clydesdale for cover. But he would not sacrifice his animal and with a swat on its hindquarters from the flat part of his sword, the proud beast ran off down the trail.

Richard was prepared to fight off a new barrage of arrows, but none came. The top of the ridge was deserted, the Indians were gone. He bent down on one knee and rolled his captain's body over onto his back – John was no more. Richard scanned his surroundings; there was nothing but wind and an occasional tumble weed. The Indian ghosts had pulled back for reasons unknown. With sword in hand, he walked a short distance to the regular's horse and pulled loose a deerskin carafe hanging from the saddle. He returned to the captain's body and drenched him with the rum the container held.

"This is the best I can do, old friend," Richard said as he pulled a match from his pocket. Striking it on his belt, he tossed it onto his friend and captain's body. Colonel Richard left his defeated army behind and headed upward, out of the canyon to the flat desert above, as smoke from the burning man rose into the sky. At some point, the wind picked up and as promised the smoke and ashes were blown across the desert toward Captain John Belien's homeland.

Richard reached the top of the gorge where he saw nothing but miles and miles of flat desert and the cowboy who stood a hundred yards off with a solid silver sword in his hand. A sword such as Richard had never seen before. He stood alone, the savages and the old Indian nowhere in sight. Richard continued at a steady walk, stopping ten feet from his foe. They stood and stared at one another for a time as clouds rolled in, blocking the late afternoon sun.

Only the sounds of the wind blowing past the huge cacti standing like guards over the desert could be heard. Richard realized this war had nothing to do with him and his army as he glared at the white collar around the man's neck. Richard spoke with wonder in his voice, "*A Preacher?*"

"Call me Jack," the man replied.

"Should I know you?" asked Richard.

"No, you should not, but in this time and place there's not much that surprises me any longer," replied the preacher.

"I am Colonel Richard Andersson, and it is my duty to slay you for the atrocities committed against my men."

When Jack heard this man's last name, it sent his mind reeling. Then he had to defend himself from the attack that followed.

Richard came forward and brought down his sword in an overhand motion, intending to split the preacher's head down the middle.

Jack was late in his defense and had to go to one knee, shifting to his right and leveling his sword overhead while blocking the blow. Metallic sounds *clanged* off the blades at their meeting; stalemate.

Richard launched straight up in a forward flip over Jack's head and landed on his feet, facing the preacher's back. Jack swung his blade behind him, rotating on his knee in a one-eighty, but Richard jumped in the air to avoid the slash, spinning in mid-flight and landing on his feet. He faced the preacher now standing in front of him at a fair distance.

They closed the gap in unison, their weapons high, battering back and forth against one another violently. The fencing style of combat went on and on. Jack began to tire and he wondered why the power of the blue light had not shown itself. He began to realize this colonel was much stronger than he, and as the fight went on, his eyes seemed to change into something less human.

Jack decided his next move. With everything he had, he pushed forward slamming his sword more rapidly and shoving his opponent backward. He suddenly stopped, took a step back, and with both hands over his head flung his sword at his opponent – there was room for one turn of the blade.

The point was a foot from hitting its mark at his chest when Richard swatted it away with the swing of his own blade. His only mistake was watching the sword's landing as it stuck in the trunk of a giant cactus. When he turned back to his adversary, it was too late.

Jack took another step back and pulled a revolver from his right hip and then began slamming his left palm down on the hammer. A silver bullet hit the colonel in his left shoulder, the second went through his left forearm.

Richard dodged, leaping and rolling to avoid the other four bullets. He went straight from the roll to a run, a blur close to the speed of a vampire. He found his Clydesdale not far away, leaped to his back,and rode off into the desert as his wounds began to burn and widen as the flesh was being eaten away.

Jack pulled his other pistol, but the colonel and his great horse had created a far distance between them. He fired two shots but neither bullet found their mark as the man and his horse had moved out of firing range.

Jack quickly reloaded then retrieved his sword. When he pulled it out of the cactus, fluid ran down its base. Jack put his mouth to it, avoiding the barbs and sucked what liquid he could get, relieving his dry mouth. Suddenly feeling a presence behind him, Jack pulled his pistol while he spun a one-eighty. As he did so, he caught a barb across his cheek, scratching through all seven layers of skin. With a deep breath, he unlocked his elbow, lowered his revolver, and released the hammer.

"Dammit, Chief, quit sneakin' up on me like that!"

White Owl said nothing.

Jack noticed the horse he sat upon had more emotion on his long face than the old Injun. In his hand, he held the reins to Jack's steed.

"Where the Hell have you been?" asked Jack, clearly irritated.

"Night comes, we must go," said White Owl.

Jack dabbed at the blood running down his face with the tips of his fingers and pulled it away for inspection. A cloud floated across the setting sun, diverting his attention. Jack suddenly did not want to be here when the sun went down. Without hesitation, he mounted his horse and followed the chief who took off at a run toward the setting sun as soon as Jack's butt hit the saddle.

White Owl was leading them to the only structure in sight, a twenty-foot-high rock formation in the middle of nowhere. Jack had never noticed the rock before, and he did feel an urgency to get there before dark. The sun was dropping fast, causing the chief to pick up the pace. Jack had to put his spurs to the stallion to close the gap.

The wind began to swirl around them as if a storm was coming. By his judgment, they should reach the big rock just as the sun disappeared over the horizon. Then what?

The horses were at full speed and Jack was right on the Indian's tail – if the chief came to an abrupt halt, they would become one. It appeared they were going to slam right into the rock face, but at the very last minute, the chief turned his horse and vanished into the rock. Jack veered off and rode past, cussing under his breath; he pulled up allowing the dust to catch up. He covered his eyes with the inner side of his forearm as the dry sand swirled around and then went past him. When the dust settled, he faced west seeing the top of the sun flattening out across the desert skyline.

The stallion began to spook, "Easy, boy, easy," said Jack as he stroked the horse's neck. "Yeah, I feel it too, boy."

The wind that blew the sweat from his face turned very cold as soon as the moon replaced the sun in the sky. *The vampires are coming,* thought Jack, *something is coming.* He rode up to the rock and put his palm on its flat smooth surface then began to move along, searching for an opening. As he dragged his hand laterally, he slid past a crevice. He backed away, steering the horse in a circle. He could now see the entrance into the formation. He understood why he missed it the first time, for he had to be at just the right angle to see it. The problem was it looked too narrow for them to fit.

The doubt left his mind as a blast of ice-cold wind blew past him. It carried the smell of death, followed by a hissing-like growl that sent a shiver up the preacher's spine. With no time left, Jack retreated from the rock, turned, and dug his spurs into the stallion's side, launching him forward. Jack closed his eyes and let out a yell as they hit the crevice. He felt four claws burn like ice as they swept the back of his neck, just before they were swallowed up by the crease in the rock.

They broke through to the other side. Jack's eyes were still shut tight, but his instincts took over, imposing on him to pull back the reins. He pulled his pistol and cocked the hammer back with his thumb, sweeping the area. The chamber was carved round with primitive paintings covering the walls. Jack transferred the revolver to the hand that held the reins and grabbed the back of his burning neck with the freed one. He felt the impression of four scratch marks, about an inch apart, running parallel underneath his hairline. There was no blood, for the scrapes barely grazed the surface.

The stallion's labored breathing slowed, along with Jack's, as they saw White Owl in the middle of the circular cavern, sitting with his legs crossed in front of a small fire smoking his pipe. Jack followed the smoke upward with his eyes, noticing that the cave was not covered. The moon and stars were shining bright, the color of blue illuminating the chamber.

Jack swung his leg over the head of the steed, sliding off the saddle to the ground, and landing on his feet. He pulled his other revolver and set the sights of both guns on the tops of the rock walls, expecting the evil he felt on the outside to enter from above. The preacher circled the area with the hammers cocked.

"Hey, Chief, they're out there. You think you could put down that pipe and give me a hand?"

"This ground is sacred," replied White Owl, without taking his eyes from the fire. "The spirits of great warriors are buried here. The evil may not enter."

Jack holstered his pistol and rubbed his neck again as the burn continued, like ice being held in one spot for too long. "Something got my neck, Chief; it's like poison, diggin' in deep."

The old Injun rose instantly to his feet and was upon the preacher before he knew it. He reached over Jack's head and pulled his sword from the sheath on his back. The chief needed two hands to manage the weight. He sidestepped behind Jack and slid the blade under the preacher's hair, pressing it flat side to the wounds on his neck. There was a sizzling sound as the blue light glowed bright.

Jack flinched slightly, but held his ground as the burn turned to relief.

White Owl stuck the point of the sword into the dirt and went back to his pipe at the fire.

Jack rubbed his neck to find the scratches had vanished. He holstered the other revolver, taking the old man's word that they were safe here, and sat down across from him. White Owl handed him the pipe, without a word.

Jack took it and drew deeply, holding it for a moment before exhaling. "What's the plan, Chief?" he asked as he handed the pipe back.

"We wait for the sun then head for the mountain."

"You're the boss," replied the preacher, as he lay back putting his head on the sand and his hat over his face; he was asleep in an instant.

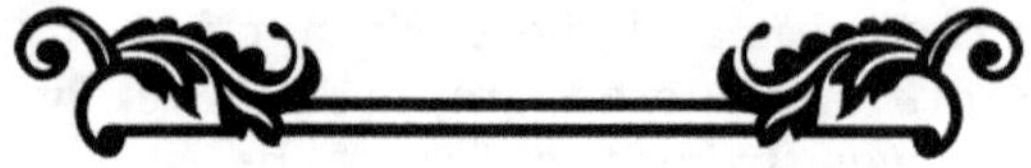

CHAPTER NINETEEN

Colonel Richard had been shot, stabbed, slashed, and beaten within an inch of his life many times over his long career as a soldier, but there was something very different about the sensation in his shoulder. The slug was lodged inside his upper body and he could feel it eating away at him like venom. He found an area with a water source as he retreated across the desert, an oasis, if you will. It was dark now, and he sat on a small flat rock, leaning back on a bigger one. The moon and stars were bright giving ample light. Richard inspected his forearm, the hole was already healing. The bullet had passed clear through and the vampire blood he had received from Andelko was doing its work.

He pulled off his top clothing to get to the shoulder wound. He pulled his knife from his belt and began digging at it with groans of displeasure. Luckily, it was not very deep. He got the point of the blade behind the slug and with a flick of his wrist it popped out and landed on the desert floor. With his gloved hand, he sifted through the sand until he found the bullet. Richard then rolled it around in his palm for inspection.

"Silver," he said. "Very clever... Very clever, indeed."

The shoulder began to heal quickly now that the silver was removed. While the colonel slipped into his shirt, the Clydesdale alerted him to danger with a snort. Richard felt the presence and left the horse behind, walking away from cover and into the open to meet Andelko. The further he drew the vampire away from the great horse, the better off the animal would be.

Richard bent down on one knee as Andelko approached him from the darkness. "I have lost your Army, Master. I have no excuse."

"You were up against powers much greater than yourself, my friend," pronounced Andelko. "The important thing is that you survived."

"I am afraid I do not share your enthusiasm," Richard replied.

"On your feet, Colonel. The Army served their purpose well, the destiny of this Earth will not be decided by men."

Richard got to his feet, relieved and discouraged that Andelko was not even a little upset that all the men were dead. Of course, what else should he expect from the undead who uses humans for a food source?

"Are you sure about your assumptions?" asked Richard. "For I met a man with powers I have not seen before."

"Tell me of the preacher and what he has to offer in this battle for the Earth."

"As a man, he has the veteran skills of a soldier with a strong heart and a strong mind. His power from beyond is the blue light, and he has help from wizards of good disguised as American Indians," Richard explained. He attempted to hide the fact from Andelko that part of his soul was drawn to this good side.

"Is there anything else?" asked Andelko with some suspicion.

Richard paused, thinking of the silver bullets, but he did not reveal this information to his master, for reasons unknown to him. "No. He managed to get the upper hand on me. I saw a chance to flee and I took it."

"Are you injured? I smell blood."

"Just a scratch, your gift of the cold body fluid heals my wounds quickly."

"Very well," said Andelko. "The coven awaits; stay on the course that the maps show and meet us at the mountain, for the time is near." The vampire turned and took five speedy steps before taking flight and vanishing into the night.

Richard gathered himself and mounted the great Clydesdale; he rode the animal at a walk toward the destination set forth. He had lost many men during his career as a soldier, but never like this. Alone and on his way to a fight which he no longer cared to be a part of, he would go on for there was no turning back. He owed it to his men to finish what they had died for and he would do so, to the very end.

♦❖♦

Chief White Owl and Preacher Jack awoke with the dawn. Logic would dictate that walking while leading the horses through the narrow cut in the rock would be the way to exit the round formation, but to Jack's dismay he watched the chief mount his horse. Jack mounted his stallion and fell in behind the chief.

"Got anything to tell me, Chief? Like some pointers or something?"

White Owl said nothing; he just took off with as much speed as he could muster in the short distance toward the slight crevice in the rock wall.

Jack winced as every bit of wisdom and common sense in his mind told him the crack was too small for them to fit. Though they had made it once, he still had doubts that they could do it again. The collision he expected did not come; the chief and his horse vanished through the crack without a sound. Jack did not hesitate; trying to duplicate the same angle, with his eyes closed and a yell, he put the spurs to the stallion and lunged forward. He came out the other side physically unscathed, but mentally he wasn't sure.

A strange feeling of being lost came over him and he opened his eyes to a sight of disbelief. *What the Hell?* went through his mind as he looked up to see The Black Mesa Mountain standing before him. Somehow they had traveled back to where the original encampment was struck at the base of the Black Mesa – with one difference, the camp was no more. The hogans were gone, the Indian women were gone, and there was not a sign that anything had ever been here at all except for Jack's wagon which looked abandoned in the middle of the sand. He saw the chief a dozen or so yards to his left, sitting on his horse, and staring in the direction of the mountain.

Jack rode over to the wagon; he wanted to touch it to make sure it was physically there. The Lord knew he wasn't sure what was real and what wasn't any longer. He dismounted and grabbed the wooden side firmly and kicked the wagon wheel. It seemed solid enough, but that's when he spotted what he was really after. Jack slid off the top to the pine box that held the bottles – only two left.

He cursed himself, *Never should have used them for target practice. What the hell was I thinkin'?* He pulled the cork and took a long swig, welcoming the burn; he pulled out the last unopened bottle and tucked it away in his saddlebag. *We will not be separated again,* proclaimed Jack in his mind. He tipped the bottle back, longer this time, as he leaned against the wagon looking over at the chief who had not moved. The only real movement was the wind blowing the white feathers in his headdress.

"Shit!" said Jack. "That's all right, Chief, you stay right there. I'll be over in a minute," he yelled. He mounted the stallion and then dug around in his flapped top pocket and pulled out a cigarillo. Striking a match on the underside of the ruffed up saddle horn, he brought the flame up to its end and inhaled deeply.

A rumbling sound came from up above. Jack looked up to the mountain from under the brim of his hat to see the purple clouds in the sky turning counter clockwise, forming an eye in the center. He wasted no more time as he rode quickly over to White Owl's side, where he would wait for the old Injun to speak.

After what seemed an eternity to Jack, he gave in; he would have to start the conversation, as was usual. "Hell of a storm," said Jack.

There was no reply from the chief.

"Well, is this it? The big show down?" tried Jack once again.

There was still no reply.

White Owl seemed to be in a trance and unable to look away from the goings on at the top of the mountain.

Jack tried once more. "Where are your braves, Chief? Shouldn't they be here?"

"They have served their purpose," replied White Owl. "They await to be set free into the Spirit World, if the Good One wills it?"

"Well, that's just great," Jack replied. Then he took another sip of whiskey. "So, it's just you and me then, against what – a dozen demon bloodsuckers?"

The chief did not answer.

Jack drank some more. "All right, let's git this over with before I change my mind." Jack corked the bottle and slid it into the saddlebag on the opposite side and re-lit his cigarillo that had gone out for lack of activity.

The chief turned to the preacher for the first time as he spoke, "I am Chief White Owl of the Navajo. I am forbidden to walk upon the grounds of The Black Mesa Mountain."

Jack pulled the cigarillo from his mouth with his thumb and forefinger with some force. "You've got to be shittin' me?"

"You must begin the ascent to make the top before night comes," replied White Owl. "You have made the climb before in your dreams. I will be here awaiting your return; if you return..."

"Thanks for the reassurance there, Chief. And you know what – I will be back, one way or the other." Jack swung his leg over his horse and slid down its side to the ground, all in one swift motion. With the sword on his back and the two .45 caliber pistols loaded with silver hanging at his hips, he walked with determination toward the base of the mountain.

"See yah later, Chief," he said without looking back, trying to sound more confident than he felt, as he got closer to the bottom of the steep path.

Preacher Jack reached the base of the Black Mesa; he stopped and looked up at the spinning storm as he pulled out his leather gloves from the duster pocket. He spoke aloud as he slipped them on, *"O Lord our Lord, how excellent is thy name in all the earth? Who hast set thy glory above the heavens. Out of the mouth of babes and suckling's hast thou ordained strength because of thine enemies, that thou mightest still the enemy and the avenger."*

The warrior preacher began the same climb he had taken in his dreams, which now seemed very long ago, to meet the evil that awaited him high on the top of the desert mountain. The storm churned over his head and covered the sun, making it seem later in the day. Jack wanted to reach the top before the night came to give him a chance to mentally prepare. He picked up the pace of his ascent. He slipped several times due to bad footing; he looked down to see he was wearing boots. In his dreams, he'd worn moccasins. This worried him, but he pushed it from his mind and continued to climb.

He pulled himself over the edge and got to his feet. He brushed the dust from his front side as he walked away from the edge toward the center of the flat. Jack looked up once again to the spinning storm only twenty-five feet overhead, holding onto his hat while pulling the drawstring tighter. The wind blew steady but eased up as he reached the eye of the storm. The eye was outlined with white clouds that turned slower than the dark ones around the perimeter. This seemed backward to Jack for the spinning should be faster at the center.

The stars shined bright in the middle of the eye, in an eerie calm sort of way. The part of the mountain where he stood was narrow from one side of the cliff to the other and the storm seemed concentrated to this one side, closer to the edge than Jack liked.

Suddenly Jack felt a chill and his breath could be seen as he exhaled.

With the smell of death upon him, came the master vampire. He flew in out of the darkness and landed ten feet in front of the preacher. Andelko was the first to speak. "You are a stubborn man, Preacher. I see you will not heed my warning or accept my offer."

"It is not in my power to forsake my Father, even if I wished to," Jack replied.

"Then you shall die, that I can promise you," said the vampire as he raised his arms.

From behind him, the coven walked out of the stormy darkness and into the starlight of the storm's eye, six on one side of him and six on the other. They moved forward as Andelko stepped back and faded into the shadows.

Jack pulled his pistols and fired from the hip.

The fangslingers fired back.

The sound of gunfire echoed like peals of thunder across the top of the Black Mesa. Jack had twelve bullets in his first load, six per gun. He fanned outward as he aimed from the center, one piece of silver for each demon until the triggers clicked empty.

The vampires growled and hissed with pain, but they kept coming and firing. Amazingly, the vampires' aim was poor and most of them abandoned the gunplay for a more traditional attack.

Jack holstered the empty revolvers and drew his sword, using both hands up and over his head, as they were upon him. With a downward motion, he split the first down the middle cutting him in half. He swung to the left decapitating another. The sword glowed with blue fire as he swung it, quickly and proficiently. A swing to the right separated the head of the third as a fourth and fifth bit down on both sides of his neck.

The white collar Preacher Jack wore flashed blue and the light ran through the bodies of the vampires, turning them to dust. The remaining demons of the coven hesitated when they saw the power of the collar and the blue light that radiated from the cross as well as the sword. The seven that still stood, male and female, began to spread out approaching him cautiously in an attempt to surround him.

Jack was forced toward the edge of the cliff to thwart their plan, moving him away from the center of the storm. He quickly realized that the eye of the storm had been helping him. As he eased away from the eye, the darker it became giving the demons an advantage in the shadows of the night. Jack took two steps forward and jammed the sword into the hard ground that was the top of the mountain; the blue light flashed in a wave of force and knocked the seven vampires off their feet, backward, and to the earth. Jack scanned left to right and back again, checking for movement. There was none.

Are they dead? wondered the preacher. *No, they were dead already.* The blade of silver stood proudly in front of him, sticking out of the ground, the hilt upright, looking like a cross marking a grave. The blue light was gone and all was quiet. The only sound was the wind and the swirling storm overhead.

Jack began to relax when out of the corner of his eye, he saw one stir, and then they all awoke. The seven vampires lay spread out in a semi-circle in front of him. Jack pulled a pistol and opened the cylinder with a snap of his wrist as he grabbed silver bullets from his belt, sliding them quickly into the chambers. He holstered the reload and did the same with his second revolver as the vampires began to roll around, some managing to get to their feet.

This time Jack would aim for the head or the heart, allowing the cross slit, silver slugs to destroy instead of wound. He began firing with the skill of a gunslinger; the first shot hit a woman just below the right eye, splitting her head open in the shape of a cross as blue fire flashed outward and then fizzled out only after decapitation.

The preacher-gunslinger went down the line, aiming for the head, and he did not miss for he did not have the luxury of another try if he were to survive. He took down four to his left before he was hit from the right. One of the three remaining vampires had reloaded their weapon and shot Jack in the hip, dropping him to one knee. Jack pulled his other revolver and with a shot to the forehead, he split the demon open in a flash of blue, while the last two fired upon him. He was hit in the shoulder before unloading his revolver in a controlled panic he destroyed the last of the coven.

Once again, all was quiet as the echoes of gunfire faded. Only the wind could be heard on the flat mountaintop. The ground was littered with headless bodies that died long ago. Some would find peace and others would not.

Jack slowly got to his feet and checked his injuries. They were only flesh wounds; one nicked his upper shoulder and the first took some meat just above his hipbone.

"You're empty, Preacher," said a voice from the darkness. Jack looked up to see Andelko walk toward him from the shadows. The demon was right, he was empty. Jack's eyes went to the blade of silver that stood ten feet in front of him, it was his only chance.

"Be my guest," said the master vampire.

Jack was already going for it; his hand had just touched the top of the hilt when the first bullet ripped through his chest, followed by another.

Andelko unloaded his guns while moving forward, the thrust of the bullets pushing the preacher backward with every shot until he was at the edge of the mountain. The vampire let out a hellacious laugh at the shock on the preacher's face; in a blur, Andelko was upon him. With both pistols turned flat in his hands, he shoved them into Jack's bloody chest, launching him off his feet and backward over the edge of the cliff.

The wicked laughter echoed across the mountaintop as the preacher disappeared into the night.

CHAPTER TWENTY

Jack was dead before he hit the ground. The loss of blood from the bullet holes, mainly the two that pierced his heart, killed him before the thousand-plus-foot-fall surely would have. The last thing Jack remembered was his prayer, asking forgiveness for his failure to his Father in Heaven. No bright light followed, no trumpets sounded – there was only darkness.

The spinning storm overhead, at the top of the mountain froze in time, the wind no longer blew, and there was only silence across the land. A miraculous sight if there was someone to witness it, but there was no one.

There came a sudden flash of blue light, then back to black; another flash of blue, followed by total darkness.

Jack's eyes opened to the blackness. He could not move for he was restrained somehow, lying on his back with his hands folded at his midsection. A white light slowly appeared with the gravelly sound of moving rock as the stone rolled away, revealing the walls of a small cave as the morning light shone through. Chief White Owl stepped through the entryway, his feathered headdress only inches from rubbing the rock ceiling making him appear taller, somehow. He carried the old case he had dug up from the desert and set it on the ground next to the slab of stone that Jack laid upon.

"I'm alive?" Jack questioned. "How is this possible?"

"Ye of little faith, Preacher," chided the chief.

Jack felt weak and slightly groggy and began to wonder if he was dreaming again. He struggled to turn his head to see what was in the ancient box the chief began to open. Jack's curiosity peaked and then turned to disappointment as he saw the box was empty.

"You've been hornswoggled there, Chief. You been carrying around an empty box," said Jack with weak laughter which soon turned into a coughing fit.

White Owl took the few steps to reach Jack and began to unwrap the preacher from his covering. He rolled Jack to one side toward him and pulled the sheet from underneath his body; he then rolled Jack away and slid the rest out from between the stone and the weight of his back. The old Injun held the woven cloth up in front of him and began to fold it along the same creases made centuries ago when it was first folded to be stored in the box.

"Lord God Almighty!" escaped Jack's lips when he saw the outline of the man imprinted on the cloth in dried blood. "The Cloth of Turin?"

Jack managed to drop his feet over the side of the flat rock and swung himself into a sitting position. He then realized he was totally naked, wearing only the cross around his neck. He rubbed his hands over the many new scars on his chest then bent his arm around and felt the rough scar tissue on his back where the bullets passed through him.

White Owl finished folding the cloth and fastened the tie downs to secure it in the wooden box.

"God has blessed me, Chief," said Jack, "like no other man on Earth. The cloth in that box is the Cloth of Turin, the very same cloth that Jesus of Nazareth was wrapped in when he was resurrected from death by Crucifixion. For the first time, my faith does not waver. I can and will defeat the evil of the fallen one's soldier."

Preacher Jack tried to stand, but he was too weak. The chief caught him and laid him back down on the slab. "You must first rest, Preacher, for time is short, nightfall approaches."

Jack faded into sleep to the sound of the stone being rolled back into place to secure him in the Tomb. He dreamed of the ravine and the Romanian soldier named Richard Andersson. It was not revealed to him who this man was or the role he might play in this attempt to speed up the end of the world. The final battle fought between the forces of Good and Evil, known in the book of Revelations as Armageddon.

Jack woke to the sound of the stone moving, followed by the appearing light. Once again, he opened his eyes to see the chief standing before him. He sat up more easily this time, amazed how quickly his strength had returned. White Owl handed Jack a deerskin pouch.

He pulled the cap and sniffed the top then took a long drink of the cool water. "Got anything stronger, Chief?"

White Owl ignored this question. "Time is short, the storm is moving again, and growing larger. The only way to stop it is to destroy the master vampire. You must eat."

Jack looked at the sliver of raw meat the chief held out to him. Jack took it from his hand to find it was still warm, which indicated a fresh kill.

"What is it?" Jack asked.

"Lamb meat, slaughtered from the first born."

"I'm not gonna' even ask where you got a lamb out here in the middle of the Arizona desert there, Chief."

Jack took a small bite half-heartedly; then another, and realizing how hungry he was he devoured the meat quickly as he could feel all his strength returning to him. Jack had been so involved with his meal he had not seen the old Injun leave the cave, but he did spot the sword leaning against the rock wall. His clothes were neatly piled on the ground with his guns and gunbelt lying on top.

Jack thanked the Lord for his meal and began to dress while thinking of the significance of the tomb and the Cloth of Turin. He knew from scripture that he had been dead for three days and then resurrected with the power of the cloth. Jack was humbled before God, taking extra time to heal with the help of the lamb.

Fully dressed now, Preacher Jack went to one knee holding the hilt of the sword in his grasp, his arms fully extended and upright out in front of him, and the sword point piercing the ground. He bowed his head and prayed aloud. As he did so, the sword glowed with blue flame.

"In the Lord I take refuge, keep me safe, O' God. Flee like a bird to your mountain. Hide me in the shadows of your wings from the wicked one who assails me. Rise up, O' Lord, confront him, bring him down; rescue me from the wicked by your sword."

Jack opened his eyes as he got to his feet and headed to the exit of the cave. Thunder could be heard rumbling in the distance. He walked through the hole in the rock to find himself standing at the side of the Black Mesa Mountain. At the same point where he climbed to the top, defeated the coven before he was shot, and was pushed to his death by Andelko. He looked to the sky, the storm had grown massively, and it was no longer just over the mountain but spread over the desert as far as the eye could see in all directions. There was no sign of White Owl, the braves, or the camp; the only movement came from Jack's horse tied alongside his wagon. Jack was by himself but he was not alone. Without delay, the preacher walked to the base of the mountain, sheathing the sword and slinging it over to his back. He slid on his gloves and began to climb with purpose, doubt and fear replaced with faith, and his strength that of a younger man.

Jack had made it a little more than halfway up when he heard the stone roll into place from the ground behind him. He turned his head around to see that the cave had vanished; only the horse and wagon remained. Jack glanced to his feet, and then smiled as he saw he wore the moccasins of the Navajo. He did not question, but allowed confidence to flood over him as he continued on until he reached the top.

Preacher Jack pulled himself over the edge, the wind attempted to separate his brimmed hat from his head, but the drawstring did its job. He moved forward toward the eye of the storm, away from the edge of the cliff. The old Injun was gone, along with The Cloth of Turin, which would surely be hidden for thousands of years. Jack knew he would not get a third chance – this must be the final battle.

Jack suddenly felt so alone, a man on top of a mountain in the middle of nowhere, fighting a battle for mankind that no one knew about. Then he reminded himself, he was not alone for good was on his side.

Thunder rumbled constantly and heat lightning flashed throughout the low-lying purple clouds of the circular storm. Jack checked the loads in his .45 caliber pistols as he walked; the cylinders were full of silver. He stopped under the eye of the storm and scanned the area as he moved the slugs from the back of his belt to the empty slots in the front, for the purpose of quicker reloads.

The bodies of the vampires of the coven he had destroyed were nowhere to be found. Jack figured they turned to dust even as their evil souls burn in the eternal fire. As these thoughts crossed the preacher's mind, he suddenly heard cries of agony riding on the wind, confirming his assumptions. Instinct took over and he pulled his pistols while simultaneously cocking back the hammers with his thumb, and turning in a backward circular motion, covering the entire area. The cries ceased with the speed of the wind and Jack put his guns away, with nothing to do but wait.

◆❖◆

Andelko Balas knew the preacher had died. He could see, as well as feel, the man's life force leaving his body as it descended over the side while falling to the desert floor below. The vampire did not pursue the preacher for he was immediately summoned inside the mountain.

Andelko had been called away to an opening on the north side of the Black Mesa, an opening that led to a pitch-black cavern a mile deep into the Earth.

The master vampire felt a presence as he entered, familiar and disturbing at the same time. The dark cavern was very hot; as he descended farther, he came to an area that opened into an ice-cold room. The presence he had touched became overwhelming and fear crept into his awareness. Fear was something he had not felt for hundreds of years and he did not like it. Doubt was also present as he saw a spinning formation of fire begin to form in the tunnel at the other end of the open room.

The light radiated from what could only be the entrance to Hell and suddenly revealed his maker, sitting on a throne of rock before him.

Andelko went to one knee and bowed his head as he spoke, "Master."

The creature that sat upon the throne was the Godless intruder that had turned Andelko into what he was, so very long ago. His eyes glowed red, his fangs were long, and horns protruded from each side of his head. When he spoke, his voice vibrated in a low growl that echoed off the rock walls, "Why does the Preacher still live?"

Andelko raised his head. "I killed him, father, but he is protected by the blue light."

"The light is the enemy," roared the evil one. The storm of fire behind him grew with his anger. "The Preacher must be destroyed if I am to reign on Earth before the written time. The Holy Spirit needs time to build his army of Angels. Eliminating the Preacher will release me from this tomb inside the Earth, and not even the White Owl will be able to defeat me."

"What shall I do, Master?" asked Andelko.

"The Preacher's neck is protected by the collar and the chest is protected by the silver cross; remove the cross and rip out the heart, devouring it will open the gates. The Preacher awaits you on top of the mountain. Go! Destroy him, my Soldier, or you will burn in the eternal fire forever."

"I will, My Master with many names; it shall be done before the morn." Andelko left the fallen one in the depths of the mountain and made his way to the top of the Black Mesa, where he would triumph and bring the book of Revelations to pass thousands of years before its inscribed time.

CHAPTER TWENTY-ONE

The storm was intense and spinning above Jack's head. He stood in the light of the eye waiting for the undead to return. The temperature dropped and a stench overwhelmed his nostrils as Andelko flew in out of the darkness and landed twenty paces in front of the preacher. They faced one another, their legs slightly spread in the gunfighter's stance. Jack threw his coat flaps behind his guns; Andelko followed suit and did the same.

"Say when, Fangslinger," challenged the Preacher.

"No, I insist – after you, Preacher," replied the vampire.

A streak of lighting struck and thunder boomed overhead. They drew their guns and began to fire. The preacher's collar and the cross around his neck glowed with the blue fire which protected him from the bullets that passed through his body. The lead from the vampire's revolvers that hit Jack flashed, and even as they struck flesh, he healed; Jack barely noticed that every shot from Andelko hit its mark.

Jack had emptied both his guns, putting Andelko to one knee for a short moment. Then the vampire's wounds mended, bringing back his wicked fanged smile. He got to his feet while releasing a wicked laugh and dropped his empty guns to the ground.

"These weapons will not decide the winner of this battle," Andelko said, and he pulled his sword.

Jack holstered his empty pistols and unsheathed the blade of silver just in time to block an overhand attack to his head. The storm continued to intensify as the two warriors dueled, trading blows at a feverish pace. Silver versus steel, good versus evil, blue and white light against red and yellow flame – the battle for Earth only they knew about. Their coats opened, flapping around them, as they spun and struck at one another.

Andelko launched upward and flipped over the top of the preacher and landed behind him with a swing to the back of his neck. Jack ducked and spun on his heel, retaliating with a level swing of his own and sliced open Andelko's abdomen. Jack straightened out of his crouch and took a few steps back, getting into his defensive stance by holding his sword high. They both looked to the vampire's midsection and watched black blood slowly seep out of the long horizontal gash.

"You're fast, Preacher, but you will have to cut much deeper than that."

"It would be my pleasure," Jack replied before he thrust forward in another attack. Blue fire and red fire flashed at the points of contact where the swords met. The dance continued with vicious intent. Jack abandoned the two-handed side-to-side action and caught the vampire by surprise, by striking with the blade one-handed in an underhand motion, catching Andelko's stomach in the same spot as before. He now had a cross cut into his belly, this second contact much deeper than the first, which had not healed – the power of the silver would not allow it.

Andelko looked at his middle with surprise as more black fluid escaped his body. The cross cut began to glow with the blue light, putting the vampire to one knee, once again.

Jack did not hesitate. He swung his blade and Andelko's sword was separated from his grip, the vampire's steel flew behind him through the air and stuck at an angle, point first into the mountain floor.

Andelko let out a growl then launched himself at the chest of the preacher, knocking Jack on his back. The air left his body quickly as Andelko pulled a dagger from his belt and swiftly cut the glowing cross from his neck, slinging it away even as it glowed.

"Now your heart is mine!" Andelko raised the dagger with both hands over his head, preparing to thrust downward into the preacher's unprotected chest,

Jack's life began to flash before his eyes, as he said, "Forgive me, Lord." Just as Jack accepted his failure, the point of a sword came through the chest of the vampire from behind – a split second before Andelko could thrust his dagger forward.

Andelko shrieked with surprise.

Jack looked behind the vampire to see the warrior Richard, holding the hilt of the steel thrust into his master's body. Without hesitation, Jack swung his silver blade as hard as he could.

Cold black fluid covered his face as the head of Andelko left the vampire's body with a flash of white and blue light. It rolled around in the dirt and came to rest upright on the neck, looking as if someone had buried the vampire there.

Richard used the sword to push the headless body off Jack. As he did, he fell to the ground face first into the dry soil.

Jack got to his feet and went to Richard. As he knelt beside him, the ground began to shake. Jack looked over at Andelko's headless body and watched it turn to dust before his very eyes. He watched the head, expecting it to vanish, but it did not; the head stared at him with fangs bared.

Jack rolled Richard over on his back; he was alive, but very weak.

"Richard, are you my brother, somehow?" Jack asked, trying to understand.

"More like great, great, great grandfather, I think…" replied Richard in a feeble voice.

"What can I do for you?" asked Jack.

"I'm not sure," said Richard with a deep cough, "The vampire blood in my veins is killing me some way, now that Andelko has passed."

Jack looked over at the upright head that seemed to be closer to them; he sensed it had moved.

Richard reached up and put his hand on Jack's chest. "Leave me, just go."

"I will not. I'm gonna' git you off this damn mountain," Jack insisted. Then, suddenly spooked, he jerked his head around. Andelko's head was at his side, trying to bite him in the leg, and as his fangs chomped up and down, the eyes glowed red.

The preacher yelled aloud in disgust and instinctively reacted. He stood and kicked the severed head with his foot. The head rolled to the center of the storm, landing upright on the neck once again. A screech came from the sky; Jack looked up to see the great white owl circling the eye of the storm before diving down and latching onto the master vampire's severed head with its talons and then flying away.

Jack watched with amazement as the great bird soared to the north, Andelkos eyes glowed red and the mouth opened and closed, showing the protruding fangs snapping at midair. Even more amazing to Jack was that behind the owl's wings, the black stormy clouds turned white and cleared in a wave as the owl became smaller the farther away it flew. The preacher made the sign of the cross with his finger and thumb at his chest. He then removed his duster and wadded it up, before placing it under the colonel's head. "You hang on, brother, I will return."

The steep thousand-foot climb down the mountain was no easy task, and would be even more difficult, if not impossible, to carry Richard without both of them falling to their death. Jack left Richard behind and swiftly made his way down the mountain to the wagon. He looked back only once to see that the skies had completely cleared.

Jack grabbed several ropes from the back of the cart and securely tied them together. Before heading back, he pulled a bottle from the saddlebag and took a well-deserved drink. He wished to bring the whiskey with him but without his coat, there was no way to do so. With the rope over his shoulder, he began his climb back up.

Richard seemed the same, no better no worse. Jack tied one end of the rope around a piece of rock; the other went around the chest and under the arms of the wounded soldier. It went fairly well until the end; Jack winced as he had no choice but to drop Richard the last fifteen feet as he ran out of rope. The colonel seemed to roll fairly well, but from this distance, Jack could not tell if there was further damage done to the man.

Jack again climbed down to the desert floor, glad to leave the Black Mesa Mountain behind forever. He made his way to Richard who was balled up on his side. Jack stretched him out on his back and checked him for new injuries, but he seemed fine other than his illness. Jack left him for the last time and hooked up Richard's Clydesdale to pull the wagon. He retrieved his stallion and tethered it alongside. He walked the wagon over to where Richard lay and loaded the weary man into the back of the cart with some effort then climbed onto the wooden bench seat.

Colonel Richard Denton Andersson, kin to Preacher Jack Denton Anderson lay unconscious in the back of the wagon as they rode away from the area. Jack didn't know where they were headed. He just knew he must get away from this place. The place where good had triumphed over evil and restored the written scripture back on its rightful path of authority.

Preacher Jack caressed the collar around his neck as he drove the wagon away from the Black Mesa Mountain without once looking back. He asked the vast desert a question aloud, not expecting an answer, "I wonder White Owl, Chief of the Navajo, if you were here, would you finally have somethin' to say about now?" After a pause, Jack answered his own question with a grin, "Nope, I'll bet not."

Amen

About the Author

Bret Lee Hart, a second generation Floridian, has spent the last twenty-five years in Marine construction; he is married and the father of two. His mother's maiden name is Emerson, as in Ralph Waldo, and on his father's side, Edgar Allen Poe can be found hanging on the family tree. With this bloodline of writers, and being named after Bret Harte from his western short stories, it was inevitable his imagination would find its way into print.

The *Half-Breed Gunslinger, Hunter James Dolin (Book II), Montgomery's Revenge (Book III), Wanted*

Dead (Book IV), and Wars End (Book V) are the five books in this "cracker Western" series, as Bret calls them, and are available at major online book retailers.

The Fangslinger and the Preacher, Preacher Jack and the Fangslinger (Book II) are also available with many other adventures soon to be unleashed from this exciting storyteller's mind in various genres, including Fantasy and the Paranormal.

Follow Bret Lee Hart on Facebook:
https://facebook.com/bretleehart

OTHER WORKS AVAILABLE FROM BRET LEE HART

~ A Paranormal Western based on the age-old battle of good versus evil ~

Master Andelko Balas is the leader of a bored, and therefore troublesome, vampire coven in Romania in the 1880s. Colonel Richard Andersson brings relief to the boredom by discovering tales of the American West and setting the coven on an exciting, but bloody, journey to a new land.

Jack Denton, reformed gunfighter, former preacher, now a drunkard, has visions of a great evil coming to Arizona as he wanders in the desert. Then he meets an Indian Chief and is given a silver sword, a special cross, and a mission. Jack is led to Black Mountain

Mesa where an unusual storm is brewing and he has to face the greatest battle of his life.

Is this the last battle for the world as he knows it? Will his renewed faith and special weapons be enough to defeat such evil?

Brief Excerpt:
Black Mesa Mountain, Arizona, 1885
He went by the name Preacher Jack, given to him by his small congregation in New Mexico. He had buried the name Anderson in the past, going by the name Jack Denton in fear of being discovered by the law, or the lawless. It was a simple life he now led, and a good life for Preacher Jack, until God's plan for him continued forward. When his wife and daughter died from disease that swept through the small Mexican village, Jack lost his faith in God and left New Mexico, wandering aimlessly, not caring if he lived or died. Forty-year-old Jack Denton, a fallen preacher, was now a faithless drunkard living off whiskey – his only thoughts were of drinking himself to death.

Forty days and forty nights into his journey of despair, Jack found refuge in an abandoned mining shack to get some rest. A vision appeared to him as he slept, the drunken haze in which he slumbered left him, allowing the vivid images of his dream to come forth...

Fear overwhelmed him as something that Jack could only describe as a demon straight from hell swooped down on top of him, baring bloody fangs to devour his flesh.

Jack Denton awoke with a scream from the dirt floor of the mining shack.

✳ ✳ ✳ ✳ ✳

The Fangslinger II

Preacher Jack

and

The Fangslinger

BRET LEE HART

~ The Paranormal Western sequel to
"The Fangslinger and the Preacher" *~*

Preacher Jack and his comrade Richard, a centuries-old Romanian soldier, thought their battle against evil was won after their climactic battle with the master vampire Andelko Balas at the top of Black Mountain Mesa. But Richard's former master was not vanquished permanently; the Fallen One has raised him up, and now Balas has an undead army at his command. The Preacher and the Fangslinger, aided by the mystical Indian White Owl and his followers, are now all that stands in the way of the vampire master's plan to empower his dark lord and unleash hell on earth.

Will the Preacher's faith be strong enough to sustain them?

Brief Excerpt:
On his return to camp, Jack was surprised to see that Richard had pulled himself up and was now leaning against a flat rock formation alongside the campsite that partially blocked the dry desert wind. As Jack got closer he could see that the color in Richard's face was much better. Jack then realized that the colonel had positioned himself in a shady spot to avoid the rays of the morning light. This concerned the Preacher, for this was something a man with the blood of a vampire might do.

"Does the sun bother you?" Jack asked.

"Slightly, yes," answered Richard, "may I bother you for some additional water?"

Jack fetched the canteen and went to one knee as he handed it over, but this time Jack did so at a greater distance.

Richard took several small sips, and then the two men stared at one another for a moment.

"You do not trust me so?"

"Ain't sure just yet," answered Jack, "you did save my life on that mountain, and the rumor is that we are kin, but the simple fact that you're hidin' from the sun does got me wonderin'."

✳ ✳ ✳ ✳ ✳

~ A Western action adventure, the first in
"The Half-Breed Gunslinger" *series ~*

In 1860 there was more open range cattle in Florida than in Texas and all the other states combined. It took a special breed of man to live there, and an even harder man to survive. Hunter James Dolin, half white and half Indian, was such a man. He was a gambler by trade and a gunslinger of necessity and attracted trouble wherever he traveled. But with his two Colt Walkers and bowie knife, he could handle almost anything.

Brief excerpt:

About ninety miles back and a few days earlier, in the crackerjack Saloon along the Withlacoochee River, Dolin's ace-high straight flush had beat one of the three outlaws' full house. He won fair and square – two ounces of gold and a just 'broke in' Henry rifle. These days that was more than reason enough to kill a man.

Hunter had felt the itch in his craw that warned him he'd out-stayed his welcome, and knew it was high time for him to leave this place. Without taking his eyes off the men at the poker table, Hunter had gathered up his winnings, while he spoke, "Thank you, Gentlemen. It's been a pleasure."

The man at the table to Hunter's left, the one who just lost his Henry rifle, had stood and replied angrily, "Do you think we're just gonna let you walk on out of here, half-breed?"

✳ ✳ ✳ ✳ ✳

Spurred by revenge...
Gunfights and gold...
One man against the odds...

Hunter James Dolin survived the revenge war of Myakka City, Florida, by killing the men who raised their guns against him and his loved ones – all but one.

The Governor directed the Army to investigate, forcing the Half-Breed Gunslinger to seek refuge deep in the swamps of the Everglades.

Hunter James Dolin was content to live the rest of his life in solitude – 'til he was sought out and told of the whereabouts of the one that got away.

This would spark a new battle of revenge, overshadowed by the Civil War, but not soon forgotten by the people who inhabit the Florida swamplands.

Brief excerpt:

Scooter was swinging like a pendulum as very large Gators came up out of the water and snapped at the chicken, just out of reach of the man's head. Scooter was screaming again, as Hunter backed Zeke up a bit, putting his face and head closer to the teeth-laden jaws of the twelve-foot reptiles. The largest of the Gators stretched his neck up and snapped two pieces of chicken hanging down less than a foot from Scooter Johnson's head.

"PULL ME UP!!!! PULL ME UP!!!!" shrieked the dangling man. "I'm not the last – Montgomery's alive! *HE'S ALIVE, PLEASE!!!"*

Hunter urged the Appaloosa forward so the rope hanging over the branch moved with him, pulling Scooter up and out of reach of the Gator's bite.

"What do you mean, *he's alive?*" yelled Hunter. "I blowed him up in his own hotel."

✳ ✳ ✳ ✳ ✳

~ A Western action adventure, the third in "The Half-Breed Gunslinger" series, set in Florida. Author Bret Lee Hart reminds us his state was once as wild as the West – and just as deadly. ~

Duke Montgomery is an Indian fighter – a hard-as-nails killer, plain and simple – who doesn't think twice about ambushing a man or killing him face-to-face. When he learns his brother Richard is dead, killed by the Half-Breed Gunslinger, Duke goes on the hunt.

To avoid trouble after his dealings with Richard Montgomery, Hunter James Dolin and the woman, Helen, travel deep into the Everglades to live in peace for a while. But, as is the way of the world, trouble soon comes looking for them.

How many will die as Montgomery seeks the Half-Breed Gunslinger to get revenge? And what surprises are in store for Hunter James Dolin?

Brief Excerpt:
"Where you headed, mister?" asked Billy.

"Myakka City is my first stop," replied Duke.

"Where's that at, Billy?" whispered Junior, leaning toward Billy.

"Not sure," said Billy, "Where's that city at, Mister? Maybe we could tag along with yah?"

There it was; Duke had just recruited these two easily with his larger mind. He grabbed the whiskey bottle by its neck, and with the other hand chugged the last of his beer then slammed the glass mug on the counter. "We leave tomorrow mornin' at sunup, meet me at the hotel. You will be paid if you do your jobs and don't git yourself killed." Duke turned and headed for the door, taking his whiskey bottle with him.

"What might our jobs be?" said Billy to his back.

The shirtless, scarred, muscle man stopped and turned after two steps. "We're going to Florida to kill a stinkin' half-breed."

Billy and Junior looked at one another and grinned with confidence that the job would be easy enough.

"What do your friends call you, Mister?" Junior asked.

"I don't have any friends, but you will call me Sir." Duke turned and walked out, leaving the saloon doors swinging behind him.

* * * * *

~ A Western action adventure, the forth in
"The Half-Breed Gunslinger" *series, set in Florida.*

While *The Half-Breed Gunslinger* fights for his life against infection from a gunshot wound, there are wanted posters being printed with his name and likeness. A $5,000 bounty on the head of Hunter James Dolin is more than enough money to attract men to the swamps of south Florida. The ending of the Civil War turns soldiers into bounty hunters as the North feels the need to cleanse the South, and men find ways to make a living.

The gunslinger's woman carries his child; Helen will need help from their close friends as her pregnancy progresses. Jebidiah and Walt will protect Helen at all costs with their experience and grit. Bodie and Bird, with their own skills, will be by their side in whatever comes their way. To their surprise, unexpected rivals come after the newly named Dolin Family.

Brief excerpt:
"What's goin' on, Hunter? Talk to me."

"Bounty hunter keeping track of our whereabouts." Helen's hand went to the butt of her gun. "Easy, woman; he's gone for now, but he will be back and with friends."

"What will we do?" she asked calmly.

"We can't stay here, it's too open. We could hold them off inside the cabin but for only so long; eventually they would burn us out. Myakka City is where our friends are; they will increase our numbers."

"Then we'll git little James, Alameda and Mocha and go to town at once."

"It ain't safe for the boy or you. I think maybe you should take little James and go with Alameda to the Seminole tribe lands..." Before he could finish, Helen was on her feet and shaking her head.

"I will not stay with that Sam Jones; Alameda can take little James and Mocha out there but I will go where you go." She turned and began walking up the bank to the cabin. "We best git packin'."

Hunter knew Helen meant to stand firm on her decision and there was nothing he could say to change her mind once she had made it. The boy would be safest with the tribe and Helen's skill with the gun would be handy. She had been battle tested and had killed without prejudice. She would be more dangerous now that she was a mother, like a mamma bear protecting her cub.

* * * * *

*~ A Western action adventure, the fifth in
"The Half-Breed Gunslinger" series, set in Florida.*

The three year Montgomery/ Dolin War was over, and not one family member named Montgomery was left alive. Hunter James Dolin had killed Richard Montgomery, his brother Duke Montgomery and their sister Jane Montgomery. The next man in line named Little Owl, for Chief of the Snake Clan of the Miccosukee, of the Seminole Indian Tribe was killed by the hand of the Half-Breed Gunslinger. Little Owl and his loyal braves were no more.

Myakka City and the James family had survived the last battle and Helen and little James were found alive at the waters' edge. Their current enemies were dead but Hunter was concerned about the wanted posters. There was no way to know how many had been printed and how far they had spread? The authors of the prints were dead but it would take time for this to be known and then believed. Five thousand dollars was a world of money and there would be men coming to kill the Half-breed Gunslinger and seeking their fortune.

Brief excerpt:
"The knife," said Hooker.

Hunter reached back and pulled the bowie from the sheath that was clipped to his pants at his back. Daryl took that too, with the same grin, only bigger.

"You take good care of that, Daryl; I will be needin' that back."

The stare of the gunslinger's steel blue eyes froze Daryl for a moment. His smile faded and then came back, but only a little.

"Oh, you won't need this no more, half-breed, not where you goin'."

"Daryl! I'm only gonna tell yah one more time to shut the hell up," the Captain warned. "Jimbo, tie his hands in the front; he's got to ride."

The big mouth drover picked up Hunter's pistol belt from the floor as Jimbo escorted the gunslinger outside. Zeke was there, and Hunter was placed on his back by two of the men.

"Where we headed, Captain?" Hunter asked.

"Daryl and Jimbo here will take you to Fort Foster and we'll let the army decide your fate."

"What of my family, Captain?" Hunter asked.

"When they are ready for travel I will personally escort them wherever they would like to go, unharmed. I give you my word as a lawman and a gentleman."

"You do as you say, Captain, and I will allow you to live. I give you my word, but your men here, a pass will not be givin'."

Jimbo glared at Hunter and Daryl laughed out loud.

"Let's go, tough guy," Jimbo replied.

"You try anythin', half-breed, and I'll kill yah with your own guns," Daryl said while resting his hand on Hunter's 44s that he now wore on his hip.

Hunter was glad to see his bowie knife tucked in the man's belt for he would need it as well on his return.